Amos Jay Cummings

Cuba and the War-Revenue Bill

Volume 1

Amos Jay Cummings

Cuba and the War-Revenue Bill
Volume 1

ISBN/EAN: 9783337378479

Printed in Europe, USA, Canada, Australia, Japan

Cover: Foto ©Andreas Hilbeck / pixelio.de

More available books at **www.hansebooks.com**

CUBA AND THE WAR-REVENUE BILL.

SPEECH

OF

HON. AMOS J. CUMMINGS,

OF NEW YORK,

IN THE

HOUSE OF REPRESENTATIVES,

FRIDAY, APRIL 29, 1898.

WASHINGTON.
1898.

SPEECH

OF

HON. AMOS J. CUMMINGS.

The House being in Committee of the Whole House on the state of the Union, and having under consideration the bill (H. R. 10100) to provide ways and means to meet war expenditures—

Mr. CUMMINGS said:

Mr. CHAIRMAN: Whenever the safety of the nation is at stake or any great national purpose is to be accomplished by war, party lines should vanish and politics be suspended. [Applause.] The war is on, and the people demand that it shall be vigorously prosecuted in the interests of the country and without regard to party interests. It can not be prosecuted without the sinews of war. This bill is drawn to furnish the sinews of war. It is a war measure exclusively, and as such I shall consider it. It contains, it is true, features which to me are distasteful. I agree with the gentleman from Missouri [Mr. BARTHOLDT] in reference to the tax on beer, and also with the gentleman from Vermont [Mr. GROUT] as to the tax on mineral waters.

The proposition to give the President power to issue bonds does not commend itself to everybody, but no war can be waged without money. I feel it to be my duty to vote for this bond proposition if all efforts to amend the bill fail. I shall vote for it all the more willingly because it is to be a popular loan. When opened, the subscription lists are to be sent to the post-offices throughout the country, and the honest farmers and mechanics afforded an opportunity to subscribe.

A popular loan, when needed, strengthens the Government. It clinches the affections and interests of the people and makes every fireside national. Such a loan stands in strong contrast with the bonds issued in 1893, 1894, and 1895, when the country was at peace with all the world. The first issue was made by private contract, giving a well-known syndicate a profit of nearly $8,000,000.

The other issue invited public competition, but most of the bonds again fell into the hands of the old syndicate, which gleaned still further profits at the expense of the taxpayers. If this proposed issue is not sanctioned by Congress, the President may be forced to follow in the footsteps of the Cleveland Administration and impose upon the country a bond issue where syndicates may prosper at the expense of the people. Money must be had, and the proposed revenue bill, aside from the bond issue, will not bring in enough money to prosecute the war. Under the law as it now stands the syndicates would reap large profits on any bond issue.

Mr. VINCENT. They will do it anyway.

Mr. CUMMINGS. No, sir; the people will come in on the ground floor. And that is where they ought to come in.

Now, Mr. Chairman, I shall do what can be done toward amending the proposed bill. The gentleman from Missouri [Mr. BLAND]

2   3543

has a plan for the issue of Treasury notes, which possibly may be feasible. Then there is an amendment proposing an income tax. It appears to me to be nonsensical. You have an income-tax law already on your statute book, but the Supreme Court has held it void. How are you going to better yourselves by reenacting the same law, so long as the Government is under the domination of that tribunal? It seems to me that the proper way would be to bring in a constitutional amendment. If the State legislatures sanctioned it, you could then pass an income-tax law which would be beyond the reach of the Supreme Court of the United States. You may be sure, Mr. Chairman, that—

The mill will never grind with the water that has passed.

The income-tax law to-day is a dead letter on the statute book. Give us something tangible, something substantial, something that will hold good after we have enacted it. An income tax, properly levied, would, in my opinion, be a most equitable tax, especially in time of war. But let us levy it in a constitutional manner.

Mr. McMILLIN. They have overridden the Constitution.

Mr. RIDGELY. I will say to the gentleman from New York [Mr. CUMMINGS] that I have an amendment to that effect before the constitutional committee. Will you help me to get it out?

Mr. CUMMINGS. I will, with pleasure.

Mr. STEELE. It may not be his amendment.

Mr. CUMMINGS. I will support it, if it is to be a constitutional measure.

Mr. RIDGELY. It is.

Mr. CUMMINGS (continuing). And I believe my constituents will support me in it, even if I do represent a district in New York City. [Laughter.]

Now, Mr. Chairman, in the Spanish Cortes to-day they are having a similar contest to that in this House. Weyler and Robledo are opposing the Spanish budget in Madrid at this very hour. I do not know what others here will do, but, sir, I never will consent to put myself in a position where I can be compared with Weyler and Robledo. [Great applause.] As a Democrat, I stand by my principles. As an American, I stand by the nation. I believe it to be the duty of every Democrat, after having made the fight that his conscience directs toward reforming this measure, to turn in and vote to give the President of the United States the power to issue these bonds, if it be necessary, to carry on the war. In doing this they sustain the vote they gave in favor of the war. In doing otherwise they stand on record as refusing to vote supplies to carry on the war which they have hailed with so much eagerness. It does seem to me that if a President elected on a Democratic platform is allowed to issue $300,000,000 in bonds in time of peace, a President elected on a Republican platform might with perfect propriety be allowed to issue $300,000,000 in time of war. [Applause.]

What I desire, Mr. Chairman, and all I desire, is to give the Executive no excuse for not conducting the war vigorously and victoriously on the ground that Congress has not upheld the President in his efforts. For one, I stand ready to vote all the supplies asked for, holding the Administration responsible for their proper expenditure. [Applause.]

CUBA.

Mr. Chairman, I take this opportunity to detail to the House the results of an investigation in March last as to the situation in Cuba. Repeatedly have 1 sought the floor for this purpose, and repeatedly have I been denied. Under the terms of the special order governing this debate my opportunity has come, and I willingly avail myself of it. This investigation was made at the invitation of the editor of the New York Journal. That newspaper had printed harrowing accounts of the sufferings of the reconcentrados, accompanied by photographic illustrations. As doubts had been expressed concerning the accuracy of these reports, the editor of the newspaper invited Senators THURSTON, of Nebraska; GALLINGER, of New Hampshire, and MONEY, of Mississippi, and Representative WILLIAM ALDEN SMITH, of Michigan, and myself, to visit Cuba and personally view the situation.

The three Senators have already embodied the result of their investigations in speeches made upon the floor of the Senate Chamber. No opportunity, however, has been afforded me to speak upon the matter in the House. All the details furnished by the Senators are correct. I wish also to add a tribute to Senator PROCTOR for his thorough description of what he witnessed in Cuba during the two weeks preceding the visit of his brother Senators. He went there of his own accord, determined to ascertain the truth by a personal investigation. His story speaks for itself. The facts detailed stand unchallenged, and can not be challenged by anyone in the least conversant with the situation.

The man directly responsible for the rounding up and starving of the reconcentrados was General Weyler, late Captain-General of the island. He was once characterized on this floor by myself as "the Gila monster of Spanish tyranny, befouling with his breath the atmosphere of civilization." This characterization is said to have touched him to the quick. He based the effort to exterminate a whole people by starvation upon the ground of military necessity. War, he declared, recognized no principle of humanity. It was not ethical, but strictly practical. Gomez and Maceo had swept from the eastern to the western end of Cuba, destroying sugar plantations and reddening the sky with blazing cane fields. Weyler retaliated in kind.

The rural Cuban was the friend of the insurgents. It was from his little patches of tilled ground that the patriot drew his supplies. The insurgents were mounted upon horses raised in the rural districts and were fed upon native cattle. The entire rural population sympathized with the patriots. It kept them supplied with information as to the strength and movements of the Spanish forces, and saved Gomez and Maceo from many a carefully prepared trap. Of course, these Cubans were noncombatant. They were not wanted in the ranks of the patriot army, as there were neither guns nor ammunition for them. They served their country best by remaining on their farms and raising yams and cattle. The revolutionary army was under strict discipline, and the agricultural population were free from marauders and predatory excursions.

Weyler was the first to recognize the fact that, while outwardly peaceful and loyal, the people were the main reliance of the Cuban army. Their friends and relatives were in the ranks of the patriots, and, more than this, they were as thoroughly imbued with a spirit of liberty as were the "American farmers in the Revolution." To use the words of a Spanish sympathizer in Havana, "The entire people were at heart insurrectionists, and the very grass under the feet of the Spaniards was insurgent."

3513

THE EFFECT OF WEYLER'S POLICY.

Weyler's resolution. once formed, was carried out with merciless severity. Martinez Campos had fought several battles with the insurgents, but was unable to prevent the invasion of the western provinces. They contained the richest plantations in the island. Maceo and Gomez had maintained themselves in front of Havana for several months. The Spaniards themselves acknowledged that they might have entered the city by a bold dash. Maceo's friends say that he was fully aware of this fact, but that he preferred to obey the dictates of prudence and remain outside.

Weyler's orders for the concentration of the rural population in the different towns were promptly carried out in Pinar del Rio. The Spaniards butchered all the horses and cattle, destroyed every hamlet, and forced the noncombatants into the different towns. The object was to render it impossible for Maceo's forces to obtain provender. In this Weyler was undoubtedly successful. Maceo's troops suffered terribly for lack of supplies. Several battles were fought with varying success. The insurgent army practically went to pieces. It was not strong enough to recross the trocha, and Maceo himself was finally killed while trying to reach Gomez with a few followers.

Weyler regarded the province as practically pacified. Meantime his edict had been carried into effect in Havana, Matanzas, Santa Clara, and Puerto Principe. Ditches were dug around the pens in various towns and barbed wire fences placed on the outer side of the ditches. The entire rural population was either butchered or driven within these ditches. No effort whatever to feed them was made. Weyler's friends declare that he meant to make provision for them, but that he was unable to do so. Meantime he concentrated his strength and marched from Havana to the border of Puerto Principe in a vain effort to bring Gomez to a decisive battle.

That wary old campaigner kept out of his way, worrying him as Marion and Sumter worried Cornwallis and Tarleton. Weyler went back to Havana. Meantime the reconcentrados died by thousands of starvation. The provinces of Havana, Matanzas, Santa Clara, and a portion of Puerto Principe were practically as free from insurgents as was Pinar del Rio. The suffering in all these provinces was intense.

Weyler began to gather himself for a supreme and final effort to drive the patriots from Santiago de Cuba, in which province they maintained a well-drilled force under Calixto Garcia. He was on the point of making this demonstration when Canovas was assassinated, and Weyler was ordered back to Spain, Blanco becoming his successor.

Weyler's friends assert that if he had remained in office six weeks longer, Garcia's column would have broken and dispersed and Santiago would have become as free from insurrection as the other provinces. In other words, the insurgents would have dwindled into predatory bands, without organization and without an attempt to maintain an insurrectionary government. The Weylerites laugh at the effort of Sagasta and Blanco to organize an autonomic government.

Certain it is that Weyler is a remarkable man. He was a military attaché of Spain at Washington during the American civil war. He served with Sheridan in the valley, and had a great admiration for Sherman and Grant. He speaks English fluently, and ought to be thoroughly acquainted with the resources and disposition of the people of the United States. He is quick in motion, alert in mentality, decisive in action, and unrelenting in purpose. At a certain hour each day he would appear upon the Prado in Havana in full uniform and march up and down the square for thirty minutes, entirely unaccompanied.

On assuming office he sent for the American newspaper correspondents. He asked how many of them had seen service in the American war. There were some who had fought within the ranks of the Confederacy, and others who served in the Union army; others had followed their profession in both armies. Weyler told the latter that they hardly needed instructions as to the news which they would forward to their papers. Their experience in the civil war had undoubtedly ripened their judgment, and they would send nothing that was improper or liable to be of service to the insurgents. As Captain-General, he had determined to do away with all censorship. As a republican, he believed in full liberty of the press. The correspondents were at liberty to send everything published in Havana and any other real news, but nothing alarmingly sensational, and nothing that they knew to be untrue. They should be cautious to give no news that would tend to disclose military plans or movements.

"Your messages will go by cable," he said. "There will be no censorship: I shall never see them until they are printed. You can wire them in the English language. I want you to understand that anything you may send of an improper nature will reflect on me both here and in Madrid, and I shall be held responsible and be censured for removing the censorship."

He told them that they were at liberty to come and see him at all times, and gave orders to admit them without formality and at all hours. Nothing, apparently, could be fairer, yet within a week the Captain-General received bitter complaints from the Spanish minister at Washington and from Madrid about the press telegrams. He was finally peremptorily ordered to restore the censorship.

CHARACTERISTICS OF GENERAL WEYLER.

Weyler's moods varied. At times he would invite a correspondent to sit down upon a sofa with him and enter into a free conversation. At others he would receive the correspondent while seated at his desk. Looking up, he would say, " Do you want to see me? Well, what is it? Speak! I am quite busy."

He spoke English only when his adjutants were not present. He seemed to be apprehensive that it would create a suspicion within their minds if they heard him conversing in English with the correspondents. If a correspondent produced a clipping from a newspaper, Weyler invariably seized it and put it in his pocket. He patronized all the clipping bureaus in the United States, and had a score of scrapbooks. All clippings of denunciation against himself were underlined with red ink. They were placed in a separate scrapbook. All caricatures of himself and of the little King of Spain were put in a different volume.

At times he was facetious. George Eugene Bryson, a well-known correspondent, once visited him and asked permission to see the *Competitor* and other American prisoners in the Cabanas. " If you don't care to let me enter the fortress," said Bryson, " please be so kind as to have them brought to the gate where I can talk to them."

" Why," replied Weyler, " don't you know that there are no

American prisoners in the Cabanas? Haven't you yet learned that I have fed them all to the sharks?"

"No," Bryson answered. "I hadn't learned it."

"Well," replied Weyler, "you don't read the New York Sun. Some days ago one of the post-office officials brought me a letter addressed to Mr. God, managing editor of the New York Sun. [The managing editor's name was Mr. Lord.] It was a good, fat letter. I looked over it and found that two bodies of prisoners had been picked up off Morro Castle with their arms and legs eaten off by sharks. The correspondent further asserted that nearly all the prisoners in the Cabanas had been fed to sharks, and the sharks had got so fat they were hardly able to swim.

"There was only one thing to do with such a letter as that," continued Weyler, "and that was to seal it up and forward it. It was a recognition of the confidence of the correspondent in the Spanish mail system. Other correspondents would have sent the letter to Key West in a special dispatch boat. Well, the Sun printed it with a flaring caption. The only regret that I had about it was that my friend Don Pancho, of the Associated Press, was beaten out of the news. But I gave Pancho a chance afterwards. On the following day I sent for him and gave him a shark story.

"'Have you heard what the sharks did to-day?' I said to him.

"'No,' he replied.

"'Well,' said I, 'this morning I sent a firing squad over to the Cabanas to shoot two Cubans. The squad was headed off in the bay by two big sharks. One of the sharks jumped into the boat and drove the firing squad to the masthead, delaying the execution until a new squad appeared,'"

He actually forced Don Pancho to send this story to the Associated Press. "And the next day," said Weyler, with a smile, "Don Pancho received a dispatch from the New York agent asking whether he was drunk or crazy."

Some absurd stories threw the captain-general into an uncontrollable rage. One day he read in an American newspaper a story accusing him of wrapping the Stars and Stripes around an American prisoner and of then burning him alive. Weyler gritted his teeth, stamped his feet, worked his Austrian chin with anger, and said that if he could catch the correspondent who wrote the story he would wrap him in a Spanish flag, place a dynamite bomb beneath him, and blow him off the island. This was said in the censor's office while a score of correspondents were awaiting a revision of their dispatches. Next day two of these correspondents disappeared from the island.

At another time, speaking of the attitude of the American press, he became sarcastic, saying that, notwithstanding their foul abuse of him, they were really his best friends and had been of great service to him. Spain was continually throbbing with indignation over the invectives heaped upon him. Editorial comments upon his course, in American newspapers, were reproduced in the Madrid press. They aroused Spanish patriotism and proved a great factor in the enlargement of his army. He wanted to thank the New York newspapers for adding at least 75,000 troops to the Spanish army in Cuba.

At one time, in apologizing for his alleged ferocity, he said he was simply obeying the commands of the Canovas ministry. He alleged that the reconcentrado decree had been drawn at Madrid

and not at the palace in Havana. He himself was the simple servant of the home ministry, loyal to Spain and determined that
she should win, even if every man, woman, and child born on the
Island of Cuba had to be sacrificed. He would make the island
a wilderness covered with ashes and bones if this would insure
victory.

"What care I," said he, with a wave of the hand, "how great
the sacrifice of life to crush out the spirit of rebellion? If I go
back to Spain triumphant, no one will ever dare to ask for detailed
accounts of the cost of victory."

A TALK WITH CAPTAIN-GENERAL BLANCO.

On March 9 the Congressional visitors, accompanied by Consul-
General Lee, paid a formal visit to Captain-General Blanco. The
party took carriages and were driven to the palace of the Captain-
General. It fronts an exquisite park in the center of the city.
Like all such palaces, it has an inner court, with marble stairways
on the right and left of the entrance. In the inner court stands a
marble statue of Columbus. Spanish soldiers in neat uniforms
guard the entrance. The party alighted from their carriages, and,
headed by General Lee, mounted the stairway, where they were
met by General Parrado, second to Blanco in command. They
were ushered into a reception room and invited to seats. The
apartment was richly furnished.

General Parrado, through an interpreter, said that General
Blanco was busy, but would receive his visitors in a few moments.
The apartment fronted the park. Adjoining it was a second
apartment resembling the governor's room in the City Hall, New
York. It contained painted portraits of the Captains-General of
Cuba for more than a century. One of the party entered this
room and was gazing at the paintings, when General Parrado
took him by the arm and began to call his attention to the most
distinguished of the group.

"De Rodas?" asked the visitor, pointing to a portrait.

"Si," answered General Parrado. De Rodas, it will be remembered, was one of the Captains-General of the island during the
ten-years war. The picture showed a clean-cut face, with a bald
head, and an exquisitely fitting uniform. After gazing at it a
minute or more, the visitor turned to General Parrado and said,
"Show me Balmaseda, please." The General, using his index
finger, pointed to a portrait on the left of De Rodas, saying "Balmaseda." This Captain-General won a reputation in the ten-years
war equal to that of Weyler in the present war. "Now show me
Lersundi," said the visitor. With alacrity the general pointed to
a portrait. Lersundi had a diplomatic face and no military air.
"Polevieja?" inquired the visitor, turning away. The general's
index finger was again brought into play. Polevieja was the successor of Blanco as Captain-General of the Philippine Islands. He
is accredited with having crushed the rebellion in those islands,
although later dispatches say that the fires of insurrection are
again burning as brightly as ever. It was said in Havana that he
is to be successor to Blanco in Cuba. Many years ago he was
Captain-General. The face bore a remarkable resemblance to that
of the late Gen. John A. Logan.

"Dulce?" inquired the visitor. General Parrado pointed to a
portrait on the opposite wall. It was that of Dulce, who was
driven from the island by the Havana volunteers because of his
clemency. As the visitor gazed upon his features and made some
remarks in English, the General looked at him querulously. Some

2543

of the Weyler newspapers had intimated that Blanco might meet the fate of Dulce. "Concha," remarked the visitor, at which the General smiled and designated the portrait of one of the most noted of all the Spanish governors. It was an American face, denoting firmness and decision. There was nothing Spanish about it.

At this point General Parrado turned, and, pointing to a portrait near by, said, "Blanco!"

"Oh, no," remarked the visitor, "not Blanco—the Prince of Wales."

At this the General laughed heartily. At the same moment General Blanco entered the room. Parrado told him what the visitor had said, and the General laughed, apparently enjoying the remark. It was a portrait of General Blanco, taken nearly a quarter of a century ago, when he was first made Captain-General of Cuba. The features were those of the Prince of Wales twenty years ago, but the complexion was darker. Blanco, however, like the Prince of Wales, has grown stout. He has a pleasant face and a mild eye. He wore neither uniform nor decoration, but was dressed in plain black. You meet a dozen men in Wall street every day who resemble him. He looked more like a prosperous banker than a Captain-General. With General Blanco came Dr. Congosto, the secretary-general. All retired to the reception room and were seated in a circle.

General Lee and General Blanco greeted each other quite warmly. It was evident that Blanco had a warm spot in his heart for Lee, and that Lee, to a certain extent, reciprocated the feeling. Each inquired after the other's health, and there was a vein of badinage in their conversation.

"You must visit me in the United States this summer," said General Lee, "and we will go to Saratoga together. The water there will be of great benefit to you. Aside from this, there are grand balls every night, and you will have an opportunity of being presented to many beautiful American ladies. I understand that during your last visit to the United States you were greatly impressed with their loveliness."

General Blanco partly understood what was said, but relied upon an interpreter for a thorough definition. Throwing up his hands, he said he feared that he would be unable to accept the kind invitation that was extended to him. "My duties might keep me in Havana," he added.

General Lee replied that if he could not find time to visit the springs, it would be his pleasure to send him several cases of the water, as he felt confident that it would be very beneficial.

AUTONOMY.

Meantime the visitor had entered into conversation with Dr. Congosto. He had met him in Philadelphia several years ago, and recalled the meeting. Congosto speaks English like an American. He was polished and cordial. He has a remarkable head, with a full, broad forehead and large liquid eyes. He is known as the Talleyrand of the Blanco administration.

"Of course your visit here is for pleasure alone?" he said.

"Hardly that," replied the visitor. "I came to see what I can see, if not to hear what I can hear."

The conversation then drifted upon the effort to establish autonomy for Cuba. The proposal, the visitor was told, came from Madrid, at the suggestion of General Blanco. The Captain-General selected the autonomic cabinet. It consists entirely of Cubans. This cabinet had complete control of the civil administration of the island, Congosto said, and they were entirely responsible for the present situation. They had removed the Spanish governors of the six provinces and appointed Cubans in their stead. One of these governors in former days had been sentenced to death. More than this, the autonomic cabinet had removed all the Spanish mayors of the different cities and appointed Cubans in their places. All the judges of the courts had been removed and Cubans substituted.

It was a system more liberal than that in Canada to-day. General Blanco did not preside at the meeting of the cabinet, and had no more power than the Governor-General of Canada. Elections had been ordered the same as those held in the Canadian provinces. They would be held some time in April. When he was asked whether the franchise was based on a property qualification, he replied, "No; the only qualification is the ability to read and write, and loyalty."

"Are the negroes to vote the same as the whites?" he was asked.

"Certainly," was the reply. "There is no distinction as to race or creed here. We recognize the negro as an equal with the whites, both socially and politically. The blacks are far more free than those in the United States," he remarked, "for if I am to believe what I see in your American newspapers, many of them are debarred from voting. In Cuba there is no feeling against them, nor any question whatever of their rights to vote."

In reply to further questions Dr. Congosto said that the inspectors and canvassers of elections were all appointed by the autonomists.

"I am told," said the visitor, "that the Spaniards will vote against autonomy."

"This may be true," was the answer; "I am inclined to the opinion that the Spaniards will carry the large cities, but that the autonomists will carry the country."

It was suggested that the autonomist elective officers might manipulate the returns so as to give an antonomist majority. Dr. Congosto smiled and replied: "You seem to be familiar with the American system of conducting elections. Here the system is an experiment," he continued, shrugging his shoulders, "but it is my belief that the autonomists will be successful."

In further conversation it was alleged that the antonomists were the ones who were making proposals to the insurgent chiefs and endeavoring to draw them within the line of autonomy. He expressed no opinion as to the result of such an experiment.

"Well, Doctor," said the visitor, "if the autonomists elect a majority and a system is inaugurated the same as that in Canada, what next? It has not received the indorsement of the Spanish Cortes."

"No," replied the secretary-general; "the last Cortes made no provision for it, but a new Cortes, under the administration of Sagasta, is to be chosen, and they will have the power to sanction it."

Here the visitor remarked that Martinez Campos had made a similar proposition, so as to end the ten years' war. It had been practically accepted by the insurgents, and Gomez and Maceo had laid down their arms and left the island with an explicit understanding that autonomy was to be given, yet when Campos became prime minister of Spain the Cortes failed to ratify it. Congosto made no reference to Campos, but replied that this proposition came from Sagasta. The elections in Spain would undoubtedly result in the triumph of Sagasta's administration. The Government usually carried the elections, and in his opinion there was no doubt about this one. A Cortes would be elected that would support the proposition of autonomy coming from the prime minister. Here the visitor said all would then remain in the hands of the prime minister. If he should change his mind and reverse his steps, the Cortes would undoubtedly vote in accordance with his wishes and refuse autonomy.

To this no reply was made, save a shrug of the shoulders. The Doctor apparently believed that none was necessary.

All this time General Lee continued his conversation with General Blanco. As the party arose they were conducted again to the apartment containing the portraits of the Captains-General. It was remarked that the Captains-General of the seventeenth century bore a striking resemblance to the signers of the Declaration of Independence. They wore queues and had clean-shaven faces. Some had blue eyes and Roman features, presenting a marked contrast to the most of their successors. General Blanco and General Lee, with General Parrado, sat down at a desk, while an artist sketched all three. The conversation rippled right merrily, with the assistance of an interpreter and an occasional sally from Congosto. It was more of a social than a formal reception.

Five minutes afterwards formal leave of the Captain-General was taken. As the party descended the marble stairway they stopped to admire the statue of Columbus. Files of Spanish soldiers still remained at the entrance.

"It was here in front of this statue," said a correspondent who accompanied the party, "that the body of General Aranguran was placed when it was brought to Havana two weeks ago. It was borne here covered with blood, amid the imprecations of the Spanish volunteers. Blanco, from the second-story window, witnessed the demonstration. With an impatient wave of the hand, he promptly ordered the corpse to be taken to the morgue. When the relatives of the unfortunate young Cuban patriot sought it, the General humanely turned it over to their care and it received a Christian burial.

TREATMENT OF AMERICANS.

The sufferings of American citizens in Cuba have been overlooked in the horror created by the execution of Weyler's reconcentration order. It resolved itself into a deliberate effort to exterminate the rural Cuban population by starvation. No effort was made to feed them. To use the words of Miss Clara Barton to a Congressional delegation visiting Matanzas, "the Turks were far more merciful to the Armenians. They put them to the sword outright and spared them the untold miseries inflicted upon the Cubans."

It was not at first generally known that among the reconcentrados driven into the Weyler pens were scores of citizens of the United States. In every case they were treated as rebellious subjects of Spain. If they protested and refused to obey the order, they were slaughtered on their plantations by the Spanish guerrillas. In most cases their cattle were killed, their houses burned, and their lands laid waste. Many would have starved to death in the pens were it not for the $50,000 appropriated by Congress. A few beyond the ken of the watchful consuls charged with the distribution of the provisions undoubtedly did die of starvation.

Gen. Fitzhugh Lee filled his functions grandly. His example was followed by Consul Brice, at Matanzas, and Consul Barker, at Sagua la Grande. All made reports of these outrages on American citizens, but these reports were buried in the pigeonholes of the State Department here at Washington. Near Sagua la Grande an American citizen was butchered on his plantation by guerrillas. The murder was brought to the attention of Consul Barker. With sleepless energy he laid bare every detail. He secured the affidavits of seven eyewitnesses of the crime and forwarded them to Washington. No reply was received, and I have no knowledge of any protest made by the State Department to the Spanish authorities.

Nor was the situation improved under the rule of autonomy. In Matanzas to-day there remains an American citizen who two years ago owned a plantation on the river, six miles from the city. He was driven into the pen under the Weyler order and his plantation destroyed. A Cuban by birth, he married an American girl in Amherst, Mass., and became naturalized. Through the kindness of Consul Brice he escaped starvation. On the 12th of November last the alleged autonomist government removed the governor of the province of Matanzas and appointed a native Cuban, d'Armis, in his place. The new governor is undoubtedly humane and sympathetic. He was once an insurgent, and was sentenced to death for treason by the Spanish authorities. He accepted office very much as Govin accepted it, with a view of again trusting Spanish promises and of giving autonomy a fair trial; but he is governor only in name.

The real governor is Molina, the general commanding the province, better known as the military governor. Molina received his commission from Weyler, and is heartily in line with his policy. D'Armis issued an order allowing the American reconcentrado to return to his plantation. The Amherst man borrowed $250 and went back to the blackened ruins of his home. He bought a scow and began to make charcoal, intending to bring it down the river on the scow. Prosperity had not fairly glimmered before his pits were destroyed, his charcoal was seized, and he was driven back within the lines.

The military governor had revoked the order of the civil governor, and the deaths from starvation, as the records show, were 1,500 a month. Indeed, 23 persons died in the square fronting the palace on the very day that the new civil governor took office. Consul Brice forwarded the facts in this case to the State Department, and a claim for damages was made against Spain. All have been buried in the archives, and not a whisper of the actual situation has ever reached the ears of Congress.

Such are isolated cases of outrages upon American citizens in the provinces of Santa Clara and Matanzas. How many similar cases have occurred in Pinar del Rio, Havana, Puerto Principe, and Santiago de Cuba the buried reports of the American consuls may faintly outline. The fact remains that Weyler drew no distinction between American citizens and Cubans when he issued his inhuman decree. Nor did he heed the protests of those consuls who were brave enough to make them. Weyler's order was positive and imperative. The language, literally translated, is:

All the inhabitants of the country, or outside of the line of fortifications of the towns, shall, within the period of eight days, concentrate themselves in the towns occupied by the troops. Any individual who, after the expiration of this period, is found in the uninhabited parts will be considered a rebel and tried as such.

In most cases the order was executed by the Spanish guerrillas, who plundered and murdered without mercy. They acted in accordance with the spirit of Weyler's order, which meant extermination, without regard to age, condition, or sex. He, as he said, simply carried out the order of Canovas, without fear or favor. It was thus, as a subaltern in the ten years' war, he carried out the orders of Captain-General Balmaceda, better known as "the butcher." Weyler shifts the onus from his own shoulders to those of the prime minister, for whom Spain alone is responsible.

THE CASE OF ZARRATE.

A remarkable instance of Weyler's firmness and unyielding spirit was shown in the case of Zabi Zarrate y Varona. He was editor of the Union Constitucional, a semiofficial organ of the Canovas-Weyler régime. Zarrate was also a captain of Spanish volunteers in active service in Havana. His aunt had been married to General Azcarraga, then minister of war in the Canovas cabinet. Azcarraga, by the way, was a native of the Philippine Islands. The brother of Zarrate was secretary to the captain-general of Puerto Rico. A younger brother was the tutor of English to the young King of Spain. For some unexplained reason, Zarrate left Havana and joined the patriot army. He carried himself with unexampled bravery and became a colonel under Maceo.

After Maceo's death he was ambushed, wounded, and captured while carrying dispatches from Pinar del Rio to Gomez, in Santa Clara. He was thrown into the Cabanas, and a court-martial was promptly ordered by General Weyler. The news of his capture reaching Madrid, Azcarraga sent a private dispatch to Weyler, urging him to treat him as leniently as possible. Weyler made no reply. He had the reputation of doing his duty, regardless of fear or favor. A private dispatch from the Captain-General of Puerto Rico met the same fate. The friends of Zarrate were in despair.

While the court-martial was in session Azcarraga sent Weyler an official dispatch, ordering the finding of the court to be kept secret. If its sessions were not ended, he ordered Weyler to suspend the proceedings and forward the prisoner to Madrid. Prompt was the answer of the Captain-General to the minister of war: "The court-martial has found Zarrate guilty of treason. The sentence is death; and if I am Captain-General to-morrow, the prisoner will be shot." Azcarraga appealed to Canovas and his cabinet and besought their intercession. They unanimously sustained Weyler, whereupon the secretary of war resigned.

Providence, however, intervened in a manner almost miraculous. The next morning the King's tutor came to the King in tears, saying that he would be unable to give him a lesson in English that day, and begging to be excused. The little King asked what was the matter. "My brother is to be shot to-day in Havana," was the reply. The King instantly sought the Queen Regent and asked her to call a cabinet meeting at once, as he wanted to make an appeal on behalf of a friend. The cabinet happened to be in session at that moment, discussing the resignation of Azcarraga. The tiny King walked into the apartment with his mother. In a neat little speech he alluded to the grief of his tutor and detailed the misfortune of his brother. There was no complaint against General Weyler. His firmness was applauded and his devotion to duty praised.

But he desired in this case to relieve the distress of a friend, save the brother, and temper justice with mercy. Never had he asked any favor of the administration, although he had been proclaimed King a long time ago. This would be his first official act. He directed that the royal pardon be promptly transmitted to Havana, bowed, and walked back to the royal apartments with the Queen Regent. The cabinet, it is said, were deeply affected by this exercise of the young King's prerogative. The dispatch announcing the pardon was sent to General Weyler without delay. It arrived as Zarrate was marching to the laurel ditch of the Cabanas, where so many patriots have yielded up their lives for the freedom of Cuba. The King afterwards complimented General Weyler, and asked him to officially inform Azcarraga and other relatives of the royal clemency. Zarrate is now an alcade under the autonomist government. This pardon, it is averred, is the only one on record that has not been promulgated through the war department in Spain for centuries.

THE COMMANDER OF THE VIZCAYA.

A story fully as romantic and interesting is told of Captain Eulate, the commander of the cruiser *Vizcaya*, the late visitor to the harbor of New York. The incident occurred in La Guayra, on the Spanish main, in 1891. The American consul there was Mr. Hanna, a relative of Hon. Jerry Rusk, of Wisconsin. The city was raided by one of Dictator Mendoza's generals. He imprisoned all of the foreign merchants and seventeen consuls, representing different nations, demanding a large ransom for their release. Hanna was out of town when the raid began. On his return he sensed the situation and took immediate steps for the rescue of his colleagues.

The only war vessel in the harbor was the *Jorge Juan*, a little Spanish ship with three small guns, detailed for coast-guard duty. Her commanding officer was Eulate, then a sublieutenant in the Spanish navy. Hanna tried to communicate by cable with the United States Government, but failed. He next tried to reach the American minister at Caracas, and was again shut off. Finally, as a last resort, he took a boat and boarded the *Jorge Juan*. Lieutenant Eulate received him with marked courtesy, and listened graciously to his story.

Hanna detailed the startling events that had occurred, and asked the aid of the Spanish gunboat in rescuing the imprisoned consuls. Eulate listened with much interest. He replied that Spain was one of the first nations to recognize the independence of the American colonies when they were struggling with Great Britain for their freedom, and she would not decline to assist the United States at a time like the present. He said his ship was at Mr. Hanna's disposal, and asked him what he intended to do. "I propose to demand the release of the imprisoned consuls," was the reply.

Lieutenant Eulate then placed thirty Spanish marines at the disposal of Consul Hanna. He ordered his crew to prepare for action. The marines were embarked in the launch, which displayed the American flag. Consul Hanna landed with them and demanded the release of the imprisoned consuls within twenty minutes, saying that if this was not done the gunboat would open fire upon the city. A single shot was fired at the Spanish vessel from the shore. It struck her in the bow, and Lieutenant Eulate responded with a blank broadside. The consuls were released under Hanna's ultimatum. He then demanded the release of the imprisoned foreign merchants. General Pepper, representing the dictator, Mendoza, promptly complied with the demand, and his troops evacuated the city. The American flag was then hauled down from the *Jorge Juan* and the Spanish ensign appeared at her stern. The marines were returned to the ship, and Captain Hanna and the released consuls warmly thanked Lieutenant Eulate for his services.

This, however, was not the end of the matter. The Spanish Government was indignant at the action of its lieutenant. He was ordered back to Havana, deprived of his command, and sent to Morro Castle. A court-martial was ordered, the lieutenant being charged with piratical acts at La Guayra. Before a verdict was rendered, the Spanish Government had officially received the thanks of nineteen foreign governments, ranging from the gigantic Empire of Russia to the Queen of Hawaii. This opened the eyes of Spain. She recognized the injustice done to Eulate. He was released from custody, was awarded one of the highest naval decorations, and placed on waiting orders. Within a short time he was made a captain in the Spanish navy and appointed chief of the arsenal in Havana.

When it was determined to send the *Vizcaya* to New York, Captain Eulate was placed in command. It was believed that his action at La Guayra would especially commend him to the American people. Spain thought that it could not offer a greater act of courtesy. Unfortunately, the action of Eulate at La Guayra had never attracted the attention of the American newspapers. The public were in ignorance of the facts. They remembered only that Eulate had presided over the court that sentenced the *Competitor* prisoners to death. When the court-martial was held up by orders from Madrid, Captain Eulate resented the action. He indignantly asked for leave of absence and went into retirement at Puerto Rico.

ANTONIO MACEO.

Of all the interesting information gleaned by the Congressional delegation, however, none is more interesting and romantic than that illustrative of the character and life of Gen. Antonio Maceo. It was gratifying to know that he was not killed by the treachery of the Spaniards, although they made several efforts to poison him. I have in my possession a pass without the lines, issued by a Spanish officer to a man charged with this mission. It is dated in 1895. The emissary reached Maceo's camp and disclosed the plot to him, begging him to be on his guard.

Maceo passed from the Province of Pinar del Rio by boat into that of Havana, and was endeavoring to reach the headquarters of the insurgents in that province, when he unexpectedly met a Spanish force and was killed. The story that he was led into an ambuscade by Dr. Zertuccha evidently is without foundation. The Spaniards liberated the physician, who was Maceo's surgeon, because he took advantage of Weyler's proclamation pardoning insurgents who should voluntarily surrender.

Maceo was undoubtedly the greatest general that the revolution has produced. He was as swift on the march as either Sheridan or Stonewall Jackson, and equally as prudent and wary. He had flashes of military genius whenever a crisis arose. It was to his sudden inspiration that Martinez Campos owed his final defeat at Coliseo, giving the patriots the opportunity to overrun the richest of the western provinces and to carry the war to the very gates of Havana.

Maceo developed rapidly in the ten years' war, which closed twenty years ago. As a boy his brightness and probity attracted the attention of General Gomez, who made him his protégé. In him Gomez had the utmost confidence, and he loved him as he loved his son or brother. Maceo entered the patriot army as a lieutenant. His promotion was rapid, and he rose to the rank of major-general. In that war he developed the ability shown in the present war. He died a lieutenant-general. No one has ever questioned his patriotism. Money could not buy him; promises could not deceive him. His devotion to Cuban freedom was like the devotion of a father to his family. All his energies, physical and intellectual, were given freely to his country. He won the rank of colonel at Sacra, between Guimara and Puerto Principe.

This was the first and the only time that Maceo was ever driven back, but the odds against him were fearful. Gomez was engaged in battle with General Valmesada, under whom Weyler learned cruelty and brutality. Gomez at this time had 800 men, and Valmesada 1,500. Only 300 of the patriots were armed with rifles. The others carried the machete, and used it with deadly effect. Two hundred men were put under Maceo's command. He was placed in an important position and told to hold it as long as possible. Meantime Gomez prepared an ambuscade for the Spaniards. Maceo held the position for hours and brought back 80 of his 200 men, 52 of the 80 being wounded. The Spanish forces were caught in a ravine and lost 600 men. It was the most momentous battle of the ten years' war. Maceo was then a captain and Gomez commander in chief.

Maceo, though a mulatto, was a second cousin of Martinez Campos. His mother came from the town of Mayari, on the north coast of eastern Cuba. Indian blood courses in the veins of its inhabitants—the Indians of whom Jesus Rabi, a prominent Cuban general, is so striking a representative. Maceo's mother was half Indian and half negro. Her family name was Grinan. Col. Martinez del Campos, the father of Martinez Campos, was the military governor of Mayari. While in this station he had relations with a woman of Indian and negro blood, who was a first cousin of Maceo's mother. It was in Mayari that Martinez Campos was born. The father returned to Spain, taking his boy with him. Campos was baptized and legitimatized in Spain, and under Spanish law the town in which one is baptized is recognized as his legal birthplace.

When Campos returned to Cuba as Captain-General he made inquiries for his mother. On discovering her residence he established her at Campo Florida, near Havana, where she was tenderly cared for until her death, some three years ago. The second cousins were on opposite sides in the fight at Sacra, in which Valmaseda was defeated. While the governments were conducting negotiations at Zanjon, under the promise of autonomy made by Campos, Maceo remained in the mountain district of Eastern Cuba. For a long time he refused to enter into any negotiations whatever with the Spanish authorities.

THE TREATY OF ZANJON.

After Maceo became a major-general and Campos became Captain-General, and while preliminaries were being discussed at Zanjon, a meeting between them was arranged. Campos was very desirous of a conference with Maceo. He sent word that he was coming, and they met on the plain of Barragua. There were two royal palms of extraordinary size on this plain, landmarks throughout the country, well known to everybody. It was agreed the two generals should meet in the shade of these palms at noon, accompanied by their staffs. The place of meeting was selected by Maceo, at the request of the Captain-General.

Maceo's army was only a few miles away. The mulatto general arrived beneath the palm trees at noon, with an escort of thirty men. Raising his field glass he scanned the horizon, but could see nobody. Surprised that Campos did not keep his word, he dismounted and found the Captain-General seated and propped against one of the palms, fast asleep. Before this discovery Maceo had seen a horse tethered in a clump of bushes 200 yards away. It had borne Campos to the rendezvous. When the Spanish general opened his eyes, Maceo said: "Why, General, where is your staff?"

"Between gentlemen, on occasions like this," Campos gravely replied, "there is no need of witnesses."

It is possible that the Captain-General did not desire the presence of his staff, preferring that the conversation should be strictly confidential. Strangers are not the only ones dogged by Spanish spies. The Government itself maintains an espionage on all of its officers.

Describing the interview afterwards, Maceo said that never in his life did he feel more ashamed than when Campos remarked that gentlemen on occasions like this needed no witnesses. In reply the patriot said: "General, pardon me," and turning to his staff ordered them back several hundred yards. Among them was the noted negro commander, Flor Crombet, whose inflexible patriotism was sometimes sullied by atrocious acts. Maceo might justly be termed the Toussaint l'Ouverture of the insurrection and Crombet its Dessalines. Saluting Maceo previous to retiring, Crombet said: "General, I hope you know your duty."

To this remark Maceo responded: "Retire, and return at 3 o'clock."

Crombet referred to a law enacted by the Cuban government similar to the one now in force in Cuba. It provided for the shooting of any Spanish officer who approached a patriot general to treat for a surrender. In telling the story afterwards, Maceo said that he saw the devil in Crombet's eyes, and feared trouble.

At 3 o'clock the escort returned, but without Crombet. Quintin Bandera, the well-known negro general of the present war, came back with the escort and reported that on reaching the camp Flor Crombet had mustered his forces and departed. This reduced Maceo's army at least one-third. Fearful that Crombet meant mischief, and knowing his savage disposition, Maceo was afraid that Campos might be attacked on his return to his headquarters. He offered to escort him back to his staff, and the offer was accepted.

Crombet had really gone to ambuscade Campos and his escort. He planted the ambuscade at a point called Los Infiernos (Hell's Steps). When Campos reached his escort, Maceo shook hands with him and departed. He warily followed the Captain-General, however, until long after sunset. About 8 o'clock at night Campos was fiercely attacked by Crombet. The attack was stoutly resisted. Maceo closed up, on hearing the first shot, and vigorously defended Campos, much to the astonishment of the latter. The assault was repelled, and the Captain-General returned to Alto Songo, Maceo accompanying him as far as Jarajuica.

Flor Crombet never rejoined Maceo. He afterwards disbanded his forces, reached the southern coast, and escaped to Jamaica. This story was told by Maceo to a friend while seated on a log on the plain of Barragua, near the two royal palms where Martinez Campos took his nap.

SPANISH TREACHERY.

Maceo had a second interview with Campos not long afterwards. It was upon the estate of an English planter. Campos urged him to follow the example of others and surrender on the promise of autonomy. Maceo stoutly refused to accept such terms. He proposed that he be allowed to secrete his arms and leave Cuba, feeling perfectly free to return to the island whenever he pleased. This proposal was finally accepted. Campos further guaranteed the freedom of the slaves in Maceo's army, promising that they should have the same rights in Cuba thereafter as Spanish citizens. He also solemnly promised that Maceo and his staff should be sent to Jamaica on a steamship furnished by Campos and there released. These promises were made in the presence of the British consul, who came to Songo with Maceo in a buggy.

On his arrival at Songo the patriot general was sent in a special train with the British consul to Santiago de Cuba. From the train he went directly aboard the ship *Thomas Brooks*, chartered to take him to Jamaica. Somewhat to his surprise, his staff was placed aboard another steamer, called *Los Angelos*. In violation of the promise of Martinez Campos, the staff were taken, not to Jamaica, but to Puerto Rico. There they were transferred to Spanish war ships and taken to Ceuta. It is probable that Maceo would also have been sent there, despite the agreement of Campos, were it not for the friendship shown him by the British consul, Mr. Ramsden, who was the owner of the *Thomas Brooks*. Some months later Campos became prime minister in Spain. He had guaranteed home rule to Cuba, but the Spanish Cortes refused to sanction the agreement. They were not, however, utterly lost to shame, for they did pass Moret's bill freeing the negroes. This, however, looked like a stroke of policy. It was evidently done to curry favor with the negroes, whose bravery, devotion, and discipline were unquestioned.

The same policy is being pursued by the Spaniards to-day. Two negroes are serving as secretaries under the autonomist cabinet. A month ago Blanco was forming a new negro regiment, offering recruits $20 a month in silver. Negro volunteers are to be found in all the large cities. The white Cubans, however, are not allowed to enter the volunteer regiments; they are invariably incorporated into the regular Spanish army. The lieutenant-colonel of the royal body guard of Captain-General Weyler was a Spanish-French negro, born in New Orleans, and once a servant of ex-Senator P. B. S. Pinchback, of Louisiana. He was a distinguished chiropodist in Havana when he was made a lieutenant-colonel. To-day he displays a dazzling array of diamonds and decorations. He is vice-chairman of the Weyler junta in Havana and chief of the colored fire brigade. He also owns a tri-weekly newspaper, which invariably reprints from the American press all the accounts of lynchings of negroes in the Southern States. In his editorial columns he alludes to them as an argument against annexation to the United States.

3513

Quintin Bandera means "fifteen flags." The appellation was given to Bandera because he had captured fifteen Spanish ensigns. He is a coal-black negro, of remarkable military ability. He was a slave of Quesada. With others of Maceo's staff, he was sent to prison at Ceuta. While in prison the daughter of a Spanish staff officer fell in love with him. Through her aid, he escaped in a boat to Gibraltar, where he became a British subject, and married his preserver. She is of Spanish and Moorish blood, and is said to be a lady of education and refinement. She taught her husband to read and write, and takes great pride in his achievements.

José Maceo, the half brother of Antonio, escaped from Ceuta with Quintin Bandera.

Antonio Maceo neither smoked tobacco nor drank spirituous liquor. When he felt unwell, he took copious drafts of orange leaf tea. It is said that he was also in the habit of taking arsenic in solution. He forbade all smoking in camp at nights, and no one had the hardihood to smoke in his presence, as he had a natural antipathy to the fumes of tobacco.

After the close of the ten years' war he became a civil engineer, and spent some years in Central America. He was in communication with Marti and Gomez, and received information of the late insurrection at Port Limon. From there he went to Venezuela and from Venezuela to Cuba. In concert with Marti, Gomez, Flor Crombet, Rabi, Bandera, and others, he assisted in organizing the army and in developing a plan of operations. The final meeting was held upon a plantation owned by a relative of the Pope. It was Maceo who planned the attack upon Martinez Campos on the way from Manzanillo to Bayamo. It was in this attack that General Santocildes was killed. Campos instinctively took an unused road and escaped to Bayamo. He had previously escaped death by strategy. He was carried in a litter from the rear to the vanguard of his army. The Cubans, taking him for a wounded soldier, allowed him to pass without firing at him.

One more characteristic incident in the life of Gen. Antonio Maceo. As the years roll by he will undoubtedly loom up as the heroic figure in the long and bitter struggle for Cuban freedom. His patriotism was entirely untainted with selfishness. His heart beat for Cuba and Cuba alone. His whole family perished in the war. No cruelty stains his record. Of unquestioned military genius, his ceaseless energy was second only to his tact and forecast. In resource he was boundless, in bravery unsurpassed, in prudence a marvel. Obeying orders himself, he commanded obedience from others. Outrages upon noncombatants were remorselessly punished. The black soldiers of Flor Crombet quickly learned to fear and respect him. Two of them were charged with assaulting defenseless Cuban women on the outskirts of a town garrisoned by Spaniards.

The evidence was clear and irrefutable. On the finding of a court-martial they were sentenced to death. In vain did Crombet and Quintin Bandera urge Maceo to pardon them. They were brave soldiers, whose reputations were previously unstained. The orders against such outrages were imperative. The strictest discipline must be maintained, and it was not a case where justice could be tempered with mercy. Both men were hanged in front of the camp, and henceforth Maceo's men were as orderly and as obedient as soldiers of Sparta. No one was excepted in camp regulations. Even the newspaper correspondents were held to as strict account in the line of march or elsewhere as the humblest soldier. Maceo was no respecter of persons when orders were disobeyed. Grave and saturnine in disposition, he had few or no favorites. Always thoughtful and wary, he never slept unless he fancied himself in perfect security.

MACEO'S MILITARY ABILITY.

Any story that sheds light upon the character and career of this extraordinary man must prove of more than ordinary interest. This incident occurred after the battle of Paralejo, where Santocildes was killed, and Martinez Campos escaped to Bayamo, leaving his routed army behind him. Flor Crombet had fallen in battle several weeks before this fight, and Marti had been killed in an insignificant fight at Dos Rios. Gomez had passed into Camaguay to add fire to the insurrection, and Maceo had been left in command in the province of Santiago. To him was Campos indebted for his defeat. He escaped capture as if by intuition. A new snare had been spread for him by Maceo after the death of Santocildes, and he was already within its meshes when, intuitively divining the situation, he came to an about face and fled to Bayamo by an unused road covered by an impassable thicket in the rear of Maceo's victorious troops.

The Spaniards were rapidly reenforced after the escape to Bayamo, and Maceo, with Quintin Bandero, began to fall back to his impregnable mountain retreat at Jarahuica. This was in the heart of Santiago de Cuba, over 100 miles east of Bayamo and 25 miles northeast of the port of Santiago. His war-worn army needed rest, recruits, and supplies. Once in his mountain fastness, he was perfectly secure, as no Spanish army would trust itself in the rocky range. News of his movements had reached Santiago, and a strenuous effort was being made to head him off at San Luis, a railroad town 15 miles northwest of that city. Nothing, however, escaped the observation of the Cuban general. With wonderful prescience he anticipated the movements of the Spaniards. His troopers were armed with machetes, and the infantry with rifles and ammunition captured at Paralejo. Bandera commanded this band of black foot soldiers.

The march had been terrific, and horses and men were nearly fagged. With sparse supplies the pace had been kept up for hours. The sun had gone down, and the moon was flooding the fronds of the palms with pale, silvery light. Maceo held a short conference with Quintin Bandera, and not long afterwards the blacks wheeled in column and disappeared. Meantime the Cuban cavalry continued its course. By midnight it had reached Cemetery Hill, overlooking the town of San Luis. The moon was half way down the sky. Maceo sat upon his horse surveying the scene below him long and silently. The little town was aglow with electric lights, and the whistle of locomotives resounded in the valley. Over 3,000 Spanish troops were quartered in the town, and their movements were plainly discernible.

Trains were arriving hourly from Santiago, bearing strong reenforcements. Through a field glass Maceo watched the stirring scene. He turned the glass beyond the town, and gazed through it patiently, betraying a trace of anxiety. Finally he alighted and conferred with Colonel Miro, his chief of staff. A moment afterwards came the order to dismount. Three hundred troopers obeyed, and were about to tether their horses when they were called to attention. A second order reached their ears. They were told to stand motionless with both feet on the ground, and to await further orders with their right hands on their saddles. In the moonlight beneath the scattered palms they stood as silent as if petrified.

Among them was George Eugene Bryson, a newspaper correspondent, who had known Maceo many years, and who had parted with him at Port Limon, in Central America, a few months before. He had joined the column just after the battle of Paralejo. In obedience to orders, he stood with his arm over the back of his horse, blinking at the enlivening scene below him. Exhausted by the day's march, his eyes closed, and he found it impossible to keep awake. A moment later he fastened the bridle to his foot, wrapped himself in his rubber coat, placed a satchel under his head, and fell asleep in the wet grass.

The adjutant soon awoke him, telling him that he had better get up, as they were going to have a fight. He thanked the adjutant, who told him there were over 3,000 Spanish soldiers in San Luis, and that it was surrounded with fourteen blockhouses. The correspondent soon curled himself on the grass a second time and was in a sound slumber, when he was again aroused by the adjutant, who told him he was in positive danger if he persisted in disobeying the order of General Maceo. A third time his heavy eyelids closed, and he was in a dead sleep, when startled by a peremptory shake. Jesus Mascons, Maceo's secretary, stood over him. "Get up this instant," said he. "The general wants to see you immediately."

In a second Bryson was on his feet. The whistles were still blowing and the electric lights still glowing in the valley and the moon was on the horizon. He went forward in some trepidation, fancying that the General was going to upbraid him for disobeying his orders. He was surprised to find him very pleasant. Maceo always spoke in a low tone, as he had been shot twice through the lungs.

"Are you not hungry?" he asked.

"No," the correspondent replied, wondering what was in the wind.

"I thought possibly you might want something to eat," General Maceo said, with a smile. "I have a boiled egg here, and I want to divide it with you." As he uttered these words he drew out his machete and cut the egg straight through the center. Passing half of it to the correspondent he said: "Share it; it will do you good." The newspaper man thanked the General and they ate the egg in silence. He said afterwards that the incident reminded him of General Marion's breakfast with a British officer. He had read the incident in Peter Parley's History of the Revolution, when a school boy. Marion raked a baked sweet potato out of the ashes of a camp fire, and divided it with his British guest. The officer regretted the absence of salt, and the correspondent said he experienced the same regret when he ate his portion of General Maceo's egg.

After munching the egg both men sat for some time observing the stirring scene in the valley below them. The moon had gone down, but in the glow of the electric lights they could see that the activity among the Spaniards was as great as ever. Suddenly Maceo turned to Bryson and said abruptly, "Were you asleep when Jesus called you?"

"Oh, no," Bryson replied, "I was not asleep: I was only just tired—that was all."

The General looked at him searchingly, and then said, "Don't worry: it is all right. We are going through that town in a few minutes. There may be a fierce fight, and you will need a clear head. The egg will give you strength."

Within twenty minutes the little column of 300 men was on the move. They led their horses down the hill about an hour before daybreak with the General in the lead. Silently and stealthily they entered the outskirts of the town. The column passed two blockhouses without being observed, and at the break of day was beyond the town on the main road to Banabacoa. Meantime the Spaniards had discovered them. The town was aroused, and 150 Spanish cavalry headed the pursuit. The road wound through fields of cane. A strong column of Spanish infantry followed the cavalry. Maceo held his men in reserve and continued his march, the Spanish troopers trailing after them like so many wild-cats. Suddenly, to their astonishment, Quintin Bandera's infantry arose on either side of the road and almost annihilated the pursuing column. Those that escaped alarmed the columns of infantry, who returned to San Luis and began to fortify themselves.

Maceo and Bandera camped on the estate of Mejorana, about 6 miles away. It was here that Marti, Gomez, the two Maceos, Crombet, Guerra, and Rabi met not long before this to inaugurate the new revolution. Bandera and Maceo found plenty of provisions at the estate, but no bread. A small Cuban boy was sent to the Spanish commander at San Luis with a note requesting him to be so kind as to send some bread to visitors at the Mejorana plantation. The boy delivered the note, and the Spanish commander asked who sent him. Without a moment's hesitation he replied, "General Maceo." The Spanish official laughed and replied, "Very well, a supply of bread will be sent. It will not be necessary for Maceo to come after it." What is more remarkable is the fact that Maceo told the correspondent beforehand that the bread would be sent, as the Spaniards had been so frightened by Bandera on the previous day that they did not want to invite another attack. That very evening the boy returned convoying many bags of bread. The Spaniards remained within the town until Maceo had rested his army and departed for Jarahuica.

SPANISH SOLDIERS.

Much has been said concerning Weyler's army. I saw many Spanish troops in Cuba. In nearly every case they were neatly dressed, fairly drilled, and usually polite and obliging. Their arms and accouterments were always in good condition, and they seemed to be in the best of spirits. They carried Mauser rifles and wore a uniform of light material, something like the old-fashioned check apron of our boyhood days. The coat resembled a Norfolk jacket, and was usually held in place by a black belt. Their hats were of a fine chip straw, with broad brims. The left side of the brim was pinned to the side of the crown with a rosette, carrying the Spanish colors. The officers wore fine Panama hats, with the same rosettes and no plumes. Their uniforms were not of the same material as those of the privates, but were of a steel-gray color. The sleeves were richly braided in gold and similar braid appeared upon the coat collar. Rank was designated by the quantity of braid on each sleeve and collar.

All the officers and many of the privates sported a profusion of medals. These were decorations awarded either for length of service or for gallantry. The most of these decorations carried increased pay, but so infinitesimal as to be ludicrous. One soldier exhibited a cross which brought in $1.72 a year in addition to his regular pay. In one case an officer exhibited an emblem granted for service in the field which produced as high as $7.50 a year. All who received honors were evidently very proud of them, whether the remuneration was great or small. Generals carried malacca canes aside from their swords. The cane is an indication of their rank. The commanding officers carry them in drilling their regiments. Besides the drill there was an inspection every morning. I saw one in Havana.

For the inspection the regiment was brought to a rear open order, the front rank facing about and confronting the rear rank. The inspecting officer started down the right of the line, the regiment standing at a parade rest. The companies came to arms port as he came down the line. From the start to the finish he held his sword in his right hand, at an angle of 45°, the hilt being within 3 inches of his nose. Each captain and ranking lieutenant attended him as he inspected their company. Occasionally he stopped and worked the locks of the different rifles with his left hand, keeping his sword in his right and still carrying it at an angle of 45°. At times he upbraided the men for negligence of attire.

Meantime the companies awaiting inspection smoked cigarettes, gazed at the ladies in the windows of the hotels, and bought tidbits from the hucksters who beset the line. The jabbering was incessant until the inspecting officer reached the company; then all were as motionless as statues. The privates seemed to look upon the inspecting officer with awe, while the company officers evidently gave cues to their men when he was approaching. There was no crowd around the regiment, and nobody, aside from the soldiers themselves, seemed to take any interest in the inspection. After the inspection the commanding officer took his station 20 feet away from the regiment and issued his orders in a loud voice. The regiment came to a close order, and moved off by the right flank at a very quick step to the call of the bugle. All the privates were young men, ranging apparently between the ages of 16 and 21.

Such was a morning scene in Havana. These soldiers were Spanish regulars. The volunteers are an entirely different organization. Their uniforms are of a different cut and texture, and they never appear in public except on special occasions. They probably drill at night in their armories. They are composed of porters, clerks, and other employees of the numerous mercantile and manufacturing establishments in Havana. Their officers are the proprietors and the sons of the proprietors. They look spick, span, and neat, and have all the élan of the national guard of the State of New York. They exhibit no disposition to enter the field in search of the enemy, but maintain their right to remain in Havana and man the fortifications, if necessary, while the regular troops are sent to the front.

Men in uniform are found on every street. The officers swarm in the restaurants, drinking light wines and feeding on olla podrida and other Spanish dishes well seasoned with garlic. There are usually ladies at their tables, and cigars and cigarettes are always in form. The generals were as numerous as generals in Washington in 1862 when Orpheus C. Kerr said that a negro threw a stick at a dog in front of Willard's and had the misfortune to spatter mud on two major-generals, four brigadiers, and twelve colonels. The Spanish generals seemed to be well supplied with money. They aired their uniforms in carriages at all hours of the day and as the sun went down appeared in profusion along a favorite drive on the seashore toward Banes.

Many soldiers were seen at country towns along the railway between Havana, Matanzas, and Sagua la Grande. When the train stopped at a depot, a corporal and twelve men were usually drawn up on the platform at a parade rest. Whether this was to maintain order or as a mark of honor to traveling officers could not be ascertained. Possibly it was to take charge of supplies shipped by train. At least half of the passengers were officers. None appeared to have passes, but all bought their tickets the same as other travelers. Each train had two ironclad cars, one immediately behind the locomotive, and the other at the tail end of the train. There were usually a dozen soldiers in each of the cars. These ironclads were provided with benches and racks for muskets. The guards amused themselves with conversation and card playing while the train was in motion. Each car was under the command of a sergeant. The trains were frequently attacked by the insurgents, although a pilot engine preceded each train a quarter of a mile.

During the Congressional visit two attacks were made between Havana and Matanzas. There was no direct assault upon the train, however. The insurgents were concealed in thickets and opened fire from ambush.

At times they used grenades filled with dynamite. The Spanish soldiers showed no lack of bravery. It was said that the traveling officers went to the opposite extreme. Whenever an attack was made upon the train they got down on their hands and knees and crawled into the ironclad cars for shelter. Many of the soldiers mounted the tops of the cars and used their rifles. In no case did they leave the trains to attack the insurgents. At nearly all stations there were restaurants, where the officers refreshed themselves with light wines and liquors.

The privates were forced to be content with their cold coffee. Not an intoxicated officer or private was seen by any member of the Congressional delegation. At one time the train passed a company of cavalry on the march. The horses resembled the marsh ponies found in Florida. The men rode in single file and appeared to be perfectly equipped. Near a bridge between Matanzas and Havana, within a mile and a half of where Ruiz was killed, there was a field battery of three pieces. They looked like old-fashioned six-pounders and seemed to be in bad condition.

The country was dotted with blockhouses, resembling those built in our Indian wars. Some were ironclad, and others protected with plank. There were loopholes in profusion. Many of these blockhouses were surrounded with ditches, like moats, the ditches being protected by a barb-wire fence and the dirt thrown up against the blockhouse. It was said that this prevented the patriots from assaulting the forts at night. In some of the houses where attacks were threatened the soldiers were ever under arms, wary, and watchful. In others they left their rifles in the racks within the house and lounged around outside in slovenly attire.

The garrisons of these blockhouses vary in size. Around Matanzas three soldiers, one of whom was a corporal, had charge of such posts. In small towns in the interior, more subject to attack, there were a dozen soldiers at each station, under the command of a sergeant.

The Spanish recruit is not boisterous nor given to horse play. He never solaces himself with songs, nor becomes particularly demonstrative on any occasion. The brightest of the recruits were called Gallegos. They are said to have a streak of Celtic blood in them, and they certainly exhibit a Celtic disposition. They are witty and quick in motion, but lack Irish brawn and muscle. The Biscayans were tall and energetic. There is said to be fine fighting material among them. This does not hold true with the Catalans and Valencians, who are more squalid and not particularly neat in habit.

Apparently there was no inspection of these blockhouses by any Spanish officials. Rarely were the guards relieved of duty, and there were no signs of drills or any military routine whatever, aside from lounging around the post and awaiting demonstrations from the enemy. Near the cities each blockhouse maintained telephonic communication with the military governor. If the soldier was in doubt concerning anything, he immediately telephoned to headquarters for instructions. I had a strong desire to visit a cave near Matanzas, mentioned by Humboldt in his travels. The proprietor of the hotel told me that I would not be allowed to pass beyond the lines.

It was useless to apply to General Molina, the military governor. Determined to make the attempt to visit the cave, I was accompanied by an interpreter, understood to be in the pay of the Spanish authorities. As we approached the last blockhouse beyond the outskirts of the city we were confronted by three soldiers in shirts and trousers, and without coats and arms, who regarded our movements with lazy curiosity. This was the garrison of the frontier fort. The barbed-wire fence around the ditch was broken down, and two hens were scratching the dirt in the little moat.

I stepped over this fence and began operations by presenting each soldier with a package of cigarettes. They were accepted with thanks. The interpreter then told them that we wanted to go to the cave beyond. They shook their heads, saying that it would be dangerous, as the blockhouse was the last outpost and there were plenty of insurgents a mile or two away. Meantime the station agent of the railway came up and joined in the conversation. He prevailed upon one of the soldiers to go into the blockhouse and telephone to the military governor for permission to go outside of the lines. He telephoned that a Federal deputy of the United States wanted to visit the cave and asked if there was any objection. It was fifteen minutes before a favorable reply was received.

We found the cave a mile beyond the lines. It had formerly been a place of great public resort, but all the houses had been destroyed, and there were no signs of cultivation. All was desolation. A broken iron stairway led down into the cave. We descended until the light grew dim, breaking stalactites and stalagmites to carry away as souvenirs. On our return two soldiers stood at the entrance. They wore neat uniforms and presented arms. They were two-thirds of the garrison of the blockhouse, one being the corporal in command. They were probably sent to prevent us from holding communication with the insurgents.

They said that they had left their post to be on hand and protect us if attacked by insurgents. Of course they were liberally rewarded, the corporal receiving a silver dollar and the private half a dollar in Spanish coin. It was the first money that either had seen in nine months.

Upon my return to the city I was met at the post by two mounted civil guards, who accompanied me to my hotel. The civil gov-

3513

ernor had learned that the "Federal deputy" had gone to the cave, and had sent this guard of honor as an escort on his return.

No signs of sympathy with the starving reconcentrados were shown by the Spanish soldiers. The starving people shunned them as they would have shunned hyenas. The soldiers treated them with the utmost indifference so long as they remained within their pens. If any ventured outside they were either shot or bayoneted, according to orders. The bayonets were short and resembled the blade of a bowie knife. The officers were far more heartless toward the reconcentrados. They sneered at them, and took apparent delight in aggravating their misery.

On returning from Sagua la Grande toward Matanzas I bought a Madrid newspaper of February 22. Although not versed in the Spanish language, I managed to extract some information from its columns. I afterwards offered it to a Spanish officer who sat in the opposite seat facing two comrades. It was accepted with thanks. Not long afterwards the officers opened a lunch basket. The car was filled with the flavor of boiled ham. Bottles of wine were uncorked, and the officer politely invited me to partake of the lunch. I as politely declined, saying that I was not hungry. As the officers finished their lunch the train entered Colon. A hundred starving reconcentrados besieged the cars on the outside, extending their bony hands in supplication and moaning for food. The savory flavor of the ham reached their nostrils.

The officers laughed at them in derision. Calling a fat young negro porter into the car, they placed him at the open window and gave him the remains of the lunch. He displayed the treasure to the eyes of the longing sufferers, and laughingly munched the boiled ham and bread, washing it down with copious draughts of light wine. To the agonized expressions of those outside he at first paid no heed; then he made up a tempting sandwich and offered it to a starving white woman, with a starving infant at her breast. As she reached forth her hand to receive it, he drew it back with a grin and ate it himself. This action aroused the risibilities of the Spanish officers, who seemed intensely amused, and patted the negro on the back.

A VISIT TO GENERAL LEE.

Consul-General Lee occupied apartments in the Hotel Ingleterra, Havana. The Congressional delegation frequently visited him. With my colleague, Mr. SMITH of Michigan, I was at General Lee's rooms on the night that the officers of an Austrian corvette were being entertained at the palace of the Captain-General. All the approaches thereto were guarded by Spanish troops. Under the order of General Blanco no one was admitted within the charmed circle without giving the countersign. It was at this banquet that the Austrian commander alluded to the trouble between Spain and the United States and assured his hearers that Austria had not forgotten the fate of Maximilian in Mexico. The remark was hailed as a threat against the United States and was cheered to the echo by the officers of the Spanish army and navy.

General Lee, after a cheery conversation, parted the window curtains and invited his visitors to a tiny balcony overhanging the street. The view was enlivening. The Prado was bathed in the effulgence of electric lights, and the statue of Isabella adorning the oblong park fronting the hotel looked like an alabaster figure. All was life and activity. A cool breeze came from the ocean. A stream of well-dressed ladies and gentlemen poured along the Prado—dark-eyed señoras and señoritas with coquettish veils, volunteers, regulars, and civil guards, in tasty uniforms, and a cosmopolitan sprinkling of Englishmen, Germans, French, Italians, and other nationalities, Americans being conspicuous. Low-wheeled carriages rattled over the pavements in scores, many filled with ladies en masque, on their way to the ball. Occasionally the notes of a bugle were heard, and anon the cries of negro newsboys, shouting "La Lucha!"

It was while watching this ever-moving panorama that the conversation turned upon the approaching war. All agreed that war was at hand and that it ought to be short, sharp, and decisive. The General knew the surrounding country thoroughly, and tersely outlined the situation. He fancied Matanzas as a base of operations. He had visited that city and had inspected the roads leading to Havana. The fortresses of Matanzas are antique and their guns of very little value. They would not stand an assault of the American Navy for more than three hours. A landing could be effected without danger and the occupation of the city made complete.

Aside from this, Matanzas is salubrious, and fully as near Key West as Havana. The air is pure and water plentiful and as clear as crystal. The city itself is within striking distance of the capitals of the four western provinces. A railroad runs to Havana; another to Guines, south of Havana, and from there to Pinar del Rio. There are at least a dozen railroads in the province. One runs direct through Coliseo and Colon to Santo Domingo, and from there to Sagua la Grande; another runs direct from Santo Domingo to Cienfuegos, and still another from Cienfuegos to Santa Clara. There is also railroad communication with Remedios, on the northern coast.

Matanzas is a little over 60 miles from Havana. The roads are good, and the railroads may be used to great advantage by invaders. An American army might approach Havana by railroad, the same as General Butler went from Annapolis to Baltimore in 1861.

With 10,000 Union-Confederate veterans it seemed to me that General Lee could capture Havana within a week after landing at Matanzas. Such a landing, however, ought to be made before the rainy season sets in. Havana has no fortifications of any account in its rear, and is practically unprotected from assault. Maceo repeatedly mustered his troops within 5 miles of the city, and could undoubtedly have captured it before the return of Martinez Campos from Matanzas. He deemed it military prudence to restrain his men. The English evidently made a mistake over a hundred years ago when they landed near Havana and laid siege to Morro Castle. Many men died from sickness who might have been saved if Matanzas had been seized and made a base of operations.

The fortifications at Havana, however, are much stronger than at the time of the English invasion under the Earl of Albemarle, in 1762. There were 10,000 British troops in this expedition, and they were only two months in capturing the city. It was the English who built the Cabanas, a fortress nearly a mile long and far more formidable than Morro.

General Lee's visitors were much impressed with his analysis of the military situation. They left him at midnight, all agreeing that it would be a just retribution for an American army corps to enter Havana with Fitz Lee at its head. His bearing in the city was magnificent. Ever wary and watchful of American interests, he visited the Captain-General's palace at any hour of the day or night whenever they were threatened.

Of course, the feeling against him among the Spaniards was very bitter, but no insulting word was ever uttered within his hearing. Outwardly all were polite, if not affable. One night, at 11 o'clock, the General was informed that a clearance had been refused to an American yacht then in the harbor. Secretary-General Congosto had told her captain late in the afternoon that there would be no trouble about her papers. Indignant at Congosto's trickery, the General seized his hat, and at the midnight hour walked down to the palace and ascended the marble steps, between the scowling Spanish sentries. In measured words and dignified manner he upbraided the Government officials for their action, and the captain of the yacht obtained his clearance papers in the morning.

SCENES ON THE ROAD TO MATANZAS.

On the following morning at 6 o'clock two of the Congressional delegation started for Matanzas. They arose before daylight, and crossed the harbor in a ferryboat that would have disgraced Hoboken a quarter of a century ago. To the left of the landing is the arena for bull fights. Crowds swarm to these fights on Sunday, and fairly revel in the brutal sport. The train was made up of five cars, first, second, and third class. Two of the cars were ironclad. The fare from Havana to Matanzas, first-class, is $13 in Spanish gold. These cars are furnished with cane-bottom seats and no racks. The windows are never washed, and the floor of the car is swept once a week. There was an improvement upon the American system in one respect—the name of the station which the train was approaching was always posted at the forward end of the car.

The railroad, by the way, is not a government institution, and no trains are run after darkness sets in. The first station out was Guanabacoa, a town which has frequently been taken by the Cuban patriots. The country was rolling and the soil quite sterile, nor was there any sign of cultivation. Spanish blockhouses capped many a hill, and the ditches along the railroad were fenced in with barbed wire. At times immense hedges of cacti and yucca lined the ditches.

Ten miles beyond Guanabacoa the train reached Minas. This was a town of a half dozen houses, containing a 5-acre pen, into which Weyler had driven the reconcentrados from the surrounding country. It was said that 800 had died in this pen. Probably a dozen starving creatures were still living. Their terror of the Spanish troops was so great that they did not dare to approach the train. Before reaching Minas a range of mountains in the south came into view.

At Minas the soil has a rich red tinge, and is said to be marvelously productive, but there were no signs of cultivation nor was anybody but a Spanish soldier seen between stations. The whole country is depopulated and runs riot in tropical vegetation. Campo Florida was the next station. It is a populous town about 15 miles from Havana. The soil between Campo Florida and Jaruco was very rich and had evidently been devoted to the cultivation of tobacco. From either side of the cars mountains could now be seen, resembling the Blue Ridge of Virginia. The country was dotted with palms. They were scattered like oaks on wild land in California or cedars in the Old Dominion. Most of them were royal palms, although genuine Florida palmettoes were frequently seen. Barren places were given up to a short palm with circular leaves and a top resembling the headdress of an Aztec chief. It is said that the seed of this palm was carried to Cuba by slaves brought from Africa.

The succeeding villages are Bainoa and Aguacate. Both had apparently been thriving places, but many of the old habitations had been destroyed. Those that remained were surrounded with miserable huts erected by the reconcentrados to shelter them from the sun. Very few of these starving people were seen, the great majority having gone to the silent land. Aguacate was near the boundary of the province of Matanzas. From this place to the city of Matanzas there is no town worthy of mention. The country is mountainous, and the mountains are covered with a scrub growth, the retreats of the insurgents. About 10 miles from Matanzas, on the left of the road, stand what are known as the Breadloaf Mountains. They rise from the plain like the Spanish Peaks in Colorado. These mountains are said to be the headquarters of General Betancourt, who commands the insurgents in the province. The Spaniards have offered $5,000 reward for his head. Several efforts have been made to secure it, but in all cases the would-be captor has lost his own head.

As the train approached Matanzas the horses of Spanish foraging parties attracted attention. The men rode marsh grass ponies laden with bales of young shoots of sugar cane that grow wild on the abandoned plantations. There were probably a hundred of these foragers, and as they spurred their steeds to the utmost speed a cloud of dust arose in their wake. The depot at Matanzas was surrounded with starving reconcentrados and Spanish soldiers. Aside from this, however, the city gave every sign of prosperity. A beautiful stone bridge crossing the Matanzas River had just been completed, and beyond it a palatial structure of light-cream material was being built.

There is no more charming spot in Cuba than Matanzas. The bay is like a crescent in shape, and receives the waters of the Yumuri and San Juan rivers, two small unnavigable streams. A high ridge separates them. On this ridge back of the town stands a cathedral dedicated to the Black Virgin. It is a reproduction of a cathedral in the Balearic Islands. The view from its steeple is magnificent. Looking backward the valley of the Yumuri stretches to the right. It is about 10 miles wide and 60 miles long, dotted with palms, and as level as a barn floor. The Yumuri breaks through the mountains near Matanzas Bay, something like the Arkansas River at Canon City. Carpeted with living green and surrounded with mountains, this valley is one of the gems of Cuba. The San Juan Valley is more wild and rugged. There were slight signs of cultivation in the Yumuri Valley, but none in the San Juan. The city itself has about 48,000 inhabitants. Nearly 10,000 reconcentrados have died here since Weyler's order, and 47,000 in the entire province, which is not larger in area than the State of Delaware. The governor's palace fronts a plaza, shaded with magnificent palms. In this plaza twenty-three persons died of starvation on the 12th of November last. This information comes from Governor d'Armis himself.

General Lee was right. No better spot could be selected as a basis of operations against Havana. A cool sea breeze is usually in circulation, and the air is soft and balmy. There are few mos-

quitoes, and encampments unsurpassed for convenience and salubrity might be made on the ridge between the San Juan and the
Yumuri. Indeed, a Spanish detachment is occupying the yard of
the church of the Black Virgin. It is surrounded by a thick stone
wall, and is a fortification far stronger than the famous stone wall
at Fredericksburg.

The Spaniards have already learned the value of Matanzas as a
military post. There are blockhouses on most of the elevations
surrounding the city, and there were no sign of disease in the detachments occupying them. The camp kettles show no lack of
food, and the soldiers themselves are clean and urbane. The
only thing that they lack apparently is discipline. Squad drills
are unknown, although the most of the soldiers are recruits lately
landed from Spain. The officers spend their time in the city
lounging around the hotels and restaurants. Fearful stories are
told of the atrocities perpetrated by a general, ferocious in aspect
and insolent in manner, who was a favorite of Weyler and who is
an intimate of Molina. The reconcentrados gaze at him in horror,
remembering the atrocious butcheries committed by him long
before Weyler's brutal order was issued. If one-half the stories
told of this man's cruelty are true, the buccaneers of the Spanish
Main were angels of mercy in comparison with Weyler's favorite.

HARROWING SCENES.

The odds and ends of the visit were instructive, pathetic, amusing, and interesting. None of the party could speak the Spanish
language, and very few Spaniards can speak English. Everyday
incidents occurred, grave and gay. Some gave rise to horror,
others excited indignation, and many threw those interested into
loud laughter. Interpreters were not always at hand, and when
on service they did not always interpret correctly. The days were
hot, with no flies, and the nights cool, with few mosquitoes.
Meals were served with neatness and dispatch, but nearly all the
dishes were tainted with garlic. You smelt garlic in the wine
shops, in churches, in hotel corridors, and on the street corners.
In Havana and Matanzas the water was as pure and clear as crystal. Havana gets her supply from river springs nearly 12 miles
away. The aqueduct was built by a Cuban at an expense of
$17,000,000. Spanish wines of excellent quality were cheap and
abundant. Not a drunken man was seen in the entire trip. No
insults were offered, and proffered courtesies were invariably
reciprocated.

The starving reconcentrado, however, was omnipresent. The
wan face and despairing eye were ever before you, and the skeleton hand was ever extended. In the streets of Matanzas and
Sagua la Grande scores of famished creatures of both sexes and of
all ages and conditions swarmed around the strangers, pleading
in low, mournful tones for food. Their appeals were as plaintive
as the notes of the peewee in northern meadows. "Madre á Dios,
Caballero"—you heard it morn, noon, and night, and the sad
refrain rang your ears even in your dreams. Misery, hopeless
misery, everywhere—whites, blacks, and Asiatics, for wherever
there is misery you find the Chinaman. Here he was conspicuous
by his silence. He stood aloof from the swarming specters, gaunt,
thin, and hollow-eyed, a picture of utter despair.

Never was his hand extended, never did he press himself upon
your attention, but there was a look in his eye that conveyed his
sense of the utter hopelessness of his situation. At Colisco a living

skeleton, with almond eyes, sat upon the platform of the railway station, listless and motionless. A battered can swung from his bony fingers. A Congressman bought two small loaves, three meat cakes, and a string of sausages and shoved them into the battered can. The skeleton arose, but there was no thankful expression in his eyes. Clasping the can to his naked ribs, he slowly moved away, but his strength was gone. He tottered and fell across the track in the hot sunlight, and as the train moved from the station there he remained, still clasping the bread to his breast. No one assisted him. No one tried to rob him of his treasure. Each re-concentrado respects the misery of his fellow.

Of the hundreds seen by the visiting strangers, not one, however pressed by hunger, made any effort to appropriate what did not belong to him. Between the squalid huts in the trochas a few tomato vines had been planted and the fruit was ripening beneath a blazing sun; yet no starving creature evinced a disposition to rob his fellow-sufferer of the product of his labor. A Spanish officer, however, strode among the huts at Colon early one morning, drew his sword, and amused himself by leveling every plant to the ground.

Nineteen out of twenty of the reconcentrados were women and children. Tots 5 and 6 years old, homeless, fatherless, and mother-less, crawled through the camps, dying from starvation. Those sent to the hospitals met even a worse fate. Upon unclean cots, with festering limbs and parched throats, they met the same hor-rible end—for up to the advent of Clara Barton they were without food and without medical relief. And the Spanish newspapers called this angel of mercy "a suspicious vulture." At Sagua la Grande one morning two bright little girls were seen seated upon the stairway leading to the office of the American consul. A Con-gressman called the attention of Consul Barker to them.

"Oh, yes," was the reply, "they are my little wards. They are the last of a family of fifteen. My heart was touched by their destitution. I found them on the verge of starvation, and am trying to save them. I found shelter for them with a family not far away, and the little things visit me every morning to show their gratitude."

They were cleanly in attire, but their faces were still pinched, and the habitual look of terror had not entirely left their express-ive eyes. Poor things! Basking anew in the sunshine of hu-manity, they were probably thrown back into the dread gulf of starvation three weeks afterwards, when Consul Barker left Cuba by order of the President.

There were very few negroes among the reconcentrados. In-deed, but one black in the throes of death from starvation was seen. This was at Matanzas. The party was returning to the city from a visit to a hospital in its outskirts. While crossing a stone bridge over the river, something like an overturned iron statue lay below, on the sward of the bank. It was the skin and bone of a gigantic negro, entirely nude. He was in the last agonies of starvation. He lay partly upon his side in the hot sun, with knees crooked and head upon his left arm. When we leaned over the parapet and addressed him, he made no reply and showed no sign of life. A moment afterwards a buzzard swooped over him, fanning his shrunken shank with its wings. And still no sign of life was shown. Again we shouted from the parapet, but the figure remained motionless. Suddenly the head was raised and the long, bony right arm moved in a feeble effort to scratch the naked thigh.

Gazing steadily at the water, in which young mullet were swarming and jumping, he faintly moaned and again assumed a recumbent position. Possibly he was deaf, for he seemed to be utterly unaware of our presence. Nor did he evince any interest when a peseta was thrown within his reach. Not far away an immense net, with thousands of meshes and hundreds of corks, was stretched upon the grass to dry. It had evidently been recently used, for silvery scales were still glistening in its meshes. When the civil guard, who piloted the party, was asked why the reconcentrados did not sustain life by catching fish, he shrugged his shoulders and replied:

"They are not allowed to do so."

"Why not?" was the next inquiry.

"Because they have no license. It costs money to get a license, and they have no money."

It was afterwards learned that the gigantic negro died as the sun went down—died of starvation, while the jumping mullet within 10 feet of him were sprinkling his wasted frame with water.

THE SUFFERING IN HAVANA.

Similar agonizing scenes turned up unexpectedly and in out-of-the-way places. There was a pitiful spectacle in the cathedral where the bones of Columbus are said to repose. The base of a statue was being built in one of the naves of the church, under which the remains are to be buried anew. A starving woman with an emaciated infant came through the doorway used by workmen and followed the Congressional party, mournfully appealing for alms.

A verger drove her into the street. Within three minutes she entered the cathedral by another door and again besought assistance. The verger was showing the party the magnificent vestments of the archbishop of Havana worn on fête days. They were sprinkled with diamonds, rubies, sapphires, and other precious stones, valued at hundreds of thousands of dollars. Across these robes the suffering creature stretched her hand, while the babe ceased whimpering and gazed at the glittering jewels as though entranced. A second verger rushed from beneath a statue of the Madonna, seized the poor creature, turned her around, and she was again driven from the church before any of the party could contribute to relieve her distress.

Another characteristic scene occurred on the Punta, opposite Morro Castle. When the heat became insufferable, two of the Congressmen were in the habit of driving to this spot to enjoy the cool sea breeze. It was flanked by an old fortification and a lumber yard, with a bulkhead and a small pier near by. A negro, naked to the waist and barefooted, frequented the place. His right leg was swollen to an enormous size. The driver called attention to the man by remarking that he had "an elephant's leg." He was suffering from elephantiasis. The foot and leg were as large as those of an elephant. One of the party threw him a handful of Spanish coppers.

Within a minute a score of reconcentrados appeared. They had been lying between the piles of lumber and were anxious to participate in the distribution. The excitement spread to others in the vicinity. Three or four wretched sufferers were sitting beneath the pier in the shade of the bulkhead. The tide was low.

They saw what was going on and struggled through the black mud in an effort to reach the Punta. One fell and was vainly trying to regain his feet when the party, overcome by the distressing sight, drove away. These poor beings had left Los Fossas, a steaming pen into which they had been driven by Weyler's orders, and were wandering about the city in search of sustenance.

INCIDENTAL

Such scenes of horror were relieved by many an amusing incident. A story widely printed of a Congressman who used his umbrella in an engagement with a company of Spanish soldiers had no foundation in fact. One night, however, this same Representative invited a colleague to ride down the Prado. A carriage was called, and an interpreter was told to instruct the driver to move slowly along the curb, giving the visitors an opportunity to listen to the music of a magnificent band stationed near the statue of Queen Isabella. The scene seemed like one of enchantment. Hundreds of ladies coquettishly arrayed, with veils drawn partly across their features, were parading the park listening to the music. As soon as the visitors entered the carriage the driver set off at full speed.

"Go slow!" shouted one of the Congressmen. "We want to hear the music and look at the ladies."

"Quiere que vaya mas ligero?" asked the driver.

"Si, si, señor," replied the Western Congressman, using the only Spanish words in his vocabulary.

The driver's whip whistled in the air, and the horse redoubled his speed. The equipage dashed down the brilliantly lighted street, and the Congressmen looked at each other in astonishment.

"Slower, slower!" they shouted.

"Mas ligero?" inquired the driver, with the sibilant "Si, si," in response.

The lash was again applied, and the speed increased until the attention of all promenaders was fastened upon the carriage. The Congressman had lost all interest in the ladies, although the ladies were evincing a deep interest in the Congressman. As a last resort the Western member arose from his seat, clasped the driver around the waist and reached for the reins. Unfortunately he secured the right rein alone, and the vehicle swung in a circle on two wheels, bringing the horse over the curb.

"That will do for me," said the Eastern Representative, as he sprang from the carriage. "I never did care much for a ride, anyhow."

His companion followed him and settled with the driver, with the remark that he "guessed he had enough." They walked three-quarters of a mile back to the Hotel Pesaje and upbraided the interpreter in unmeasured terms. It turned out that he had told the driver to take the party to some place of amusement, as they wanted to hear music. It was after 9 o'clock and the driver was anxious to arrive at a music hall before it closed for the night. Of course he understood not a word of English. When told to go slower he asked if he should go faster. The "Si, si" of the Western Congressman confirmed him in his belief, and he was utterly dumfounded when the reins were seized and the visitors disembarked.

Another amusing incident occurred while these two Congressmen were dining in a restaurant. At an adjoining table sat two Spanish officers. They glared savagely at the two strangers, jabbering meanwhile in vigorous Spanish. The Congressmen, fancying that they were the subject of conversation, became indignant.

"I believe," said one of them, "that these fellows are calling us American pigs and using other insulting terms. I have half a mind to walk over to them and demand an explanation." He was about to do something rash when a Scotchman, who sat at the table, smiled and said:

" You make a mistake. The gentlemen are not referring to you in any manner. The heavy man is damning his shoes, saying that they pinch his feet and give him great pain. His friend is advising him to sell them and have a pair made by a Havana shoemaker."

Both had drawn their shoes from the quartermaster's department on the previous day. The small officer had exchanged his with a shopkeeper and was advising his comrade to follow his example.

THE CUBAN PATRIOTS.

No one but Maximo Gomez himself knows the exact strength of the Cuban army. The bulk of the enrolled force is quartered in the provinces of Santiago de Cuba and Puerto Principe. There are scattering detachments under different leaders in Santa Clara, Matanzas, Havana, and Pinar del Rio. Each little city has its own little junta, who distributes Gomez's orders and pronunciamentos throughout the island. I was visited by a member of one of these juntas while in an interior city. The interview was arranged by an American who had spent several years in the island.

I was enjoying a siesta in my room after dinner, when the door was opened and the secretary of the little rural junta popped in without warning. Knowing the number of the room, he had escaped observation in the hotel, slipped up the stone stairway, and entered the apartment without being seen. The lattices opening on the balcony were closed, and after ascertaining the absence of all eavesdroppers, the door was locked. The windows fronted the main street, and only the plaintive cries of starving reconcentrados outside reached the ear. In the darkened room the conversation was carried on in low tones.

Much information was gleaned on both sides. The secretary listened with breathless interest to an analysis of the situation in the United States. He spoke English very imperfectly, but seemed to have no difficulty in understanding it. When told that President McKinley's determination to put a stop to the Spanish atrocities was fixed and unalterable, and that the American people were in a warlike fever over the destruction of the *Maine*, he shook his head doubtfully. He spoke of hopes blasted in the past, and evidently had little faith in the future. The information that Congress had put $50,000,000 in the hands of the President to prepare for war dazed him.

Then his black eyes began to snap, and he ran his fingers through his hair. He could scarcely believe his ears when told that the Americans took no more stock in autonomy than did the Cubans. Their failure to either recognize the independence of the island republic, or to grant the patriots even belligerent rights, made him feel still despondent. He feared that it foreshadowed a determination to annex the island. Assured that the sentiment in Washington was against annexation, he replied: " If true, that is glorious news. It will cheer Gomez, and in case of war secure the hearty cooperation of his troops." With this opening, he was asked how many troops Gomez could bring into the field.

35

As he was about to reply something heavy fell with a crash outside the door. In an instant he sprang to his feet, quivering with apprehension. I opened the door. A music rack had fallen to the floor. It had probably been blown over by the wind, which came from the courtyard in breezy puffs, imparting a delicious coolness to the atmosphere. But the secretary was not to be reassured. He was pale and nervous and was confident that some one had been listening at the door. For a minute or more he was mute and motionless. The wind rattled the bars of the lattice. "The balcony, the balcony!" he whispered. "Some one is on the balcony!"

I threw open the latticed doors, while the Cuban shrank behind the curtain of the bed. There was no cause for alarm. The street below was dotted with Spanish soldiers, but none of them had found his way to the balcony. The cries of the poor reconcentrados were more plaintive than ever. One scene photographed itself upon my memory. A man with two heads of lettuce was passing the hotel. A starving girl in rags implored him for food. She was white-lipped and thin; there was burning fever in her veins. The citizen broke off a leaf of the lettuce and placed it in her bony fingers.

She had hardly raised it to her lips before the man was fairly mobbed by famishing creatures. Among them was a crippled boy. Crawling along the curb, he clasped his arms around the legs of the man and moaned pitifully. In a second he was kicked into the gutter. The citizen fought his way to the corner and disappeared with his lettuce, while Spanish officers in undress uniform brandished their malacca canes and roared with laughter. A moment afterwards the sufferers were driven to cover by a spiteful sputter of Spanish profanity.

Again was the lattice closed and the Cuban assured that there was no foundation for his suspicions. He replied that the American visitors were surrounded by Spanish spies. Every movement was watched, and those who called upon them were marked men. Even the servants in their rooms were in the employ of the Government. "There's some truth in this, I reckon," I returned. "I have made the acquaintance of my spy. He's a good-natured Irishman, who speaks Spanish like a native and drinks whisky like a Kentuckian. Everybody tells me he's a spy and gives him the cold shoulder, but I find him very useful and hope to retain his services."

The delegate from the junta, however, was in no good mood for badinage. He resumed his seat with evident trepidation, saying that he had important papers in his pockets. If found upon him by the Spaniards, they might lead to his imprisonment and death. He then drew from his coat pocket a small printed proclamation or order signed by Maximo Gomez. It was printed in Spanish and was not larger than the leaf of a prayer book. This proclamation or order was to be placed in the hands of General Betancourt before sundown on the succeeding day. Betancourt was in the mountains near the coast, and the delegate from the junta was charged with the delivery of the order.

Before twenty-four hours a similar document would reach General Bermudez in Santa Clara, General Rodriguez in Havana, and General Delgado in Pinar del Rio. It was of great importance, and the representative of the junta seemed burdened with a sense of his responsibility. He tried to translate the document, but was utterly unable to make himself understood. One of the Congressional party was a United States Senator who had some knowledge of the Spanish language. He was sent for, and as he entered the room and was introduced to the Cuban visitor I passed him the order of General Gomez and asked him what he thought of it.

Evidently the Senator had not corralled enough of the Spanish vocabulary to make a free translation. Besides, his eyesight was bad, and there was no sunlight in the apartment. He floundered through it with difficulty and finally gave it up altogether. Apparently he did not consider it a document of transcendent importance, for he laid it on the table and began to talk on other subjects. The Cuban was once more questioned concerning the strength of the insurgents in the field. Although extremely well informed, he placed the figures rather high. They did not correspond with figures gleaned from sources equally trustworthy. He credited Gen. Perico Delgado, in the western province, with nearly 2,000 men. Vidal Ducasse, second in command, had been killed only ten days before, but his brother still had a hardy force which was hanging on the flanks of the Spanish troops and doing good service.

It was Delgado, by the way, to whom Captain Dorst, of the American Army, carried a shipload of arms and ammunition. Dorst had a fight with the Spaniards, killing two of them, but the expedition was successful in only a limited degree, and was hardly satisfactory. The result shows that Delgado had not more than a quarter of the force with which he was credited. Indeed, it is difficult to see how he could provision even 600 men. Weyler killed every horse, mule, ox, cow, sheep, and hog in Pinar del Rio, and destroyed every hut and hacienda.

Nothing living was left alive except the buzzards, now styled "Weyler's chickens." Nothing that could give shelter was allowed to stand. In no province on the island was the reconcentrado order more ruthlessly carried out. Fire and sword were rampant, and the whole country, aside from the railroad towns, became a wilderness. "Even the grass beneath our feet was insurgent," to use the words of a Spanish staff officer, and Weyler would have stamped out vegetation itself if possible. It was a horrible state of affairs, even at the outset—so horrible that it sent Maceo across the trocha over a year ago in search of relief. It was the expedition in which he lost his life.

As to the Province of Havana the junta representative was equally positive and no more specific. He was certain that General Rodriguez had fully as many men as Delgado. This was undoubtedly true, but their united force was nearer 1,200 than 4,000. The same state of destitution existed in this province as in Pinar del Rio, and it was impossible to subsist a large body of men. The most of the patriots in arms here foraged in the markets of Havana. Provisions were sent to them regularly and their underground railroad was as safe and in as active operation as the one in use between the North and South before the war. Nestor Aranguren had been the lieutenant of General Rodriguez. His death, only a fortnight before, ended as romantic an incident as the death of Major André in the Revolutionary war. Colonel Ruiz, a Spanish officer, visited Aranguren, who was an intimate friend, and urged him to accept autonomy and lay down his arms. Aranguren warned him against making such propositions when they first met.

The order from Gomez was to shoot anybody who made any such proposal. Aranguren carried out these orders to the letter.

Ruiz was executed within a mile of the railroad between Havana and Matanzas. Within a month, however, the Spaniards captured a negro who was a trusted servant of Aranguren. They threatened him with death unless he disclosed his master's retreat, and promised him a reward of 500 silver dollars if he would betray him. Aranguren was surprised in a cabin by two Spanish regiments in the early morning and killed.

As to the Province of Matanzas, the Cuban at first asserted that General Betancourt had an army of 4,000 men. When told that this was ridiculous, he reduced the number to 1,400. It is doubtful, however, whether the General had 700 men. Betancourt, like Aranguren, is a scion of one of the first Cuban families. He was educated abroad and speaks seven different languages. He is fully as daring as Aranguren and is said to have made many a midnight visit to Matanzas. He probably secured provisions and ammunition for his men during these midnight excursions. The Spanish soldiers were nine months in arrears of pay and sold their cartridges for cash to any purchaser.

In the province of Santa Clara General Bermudez was said to be in command. His reputation for ferocity tarnished his reputation for bravery. During the Congressional visit two Spanish officers sought an interview with a Colonel Nunez, under his command. They were surprised by Bermudez himself, who ordered their immediate execution. They met their fate bravely, and were buried at Esperanza on the day the Congressional delegation passed through that city. It was said that Bermudez had at least 3,000 troops under his command. The figures were far too high. He probably had not one-third of this number. The province of Santa Clara was utterly destitute of provisions. The city of Santa Clara was supplied by railroad, but the country was ravaged and ruined by Spanish guerrillas, who were employed to carry out Weyler's orders. Over 7,500 reconcentrados died in the city within four months. These figures come from the mayor.

In Puerto Principe Gomez himself was located in the mountains 20 miles from the northern shore. Further south Quintin Bandera held mountain sway. Bandera's force was estimated at 1,700. It was far too great an estimate. Gomez himself usually had no more than 300 men with him. The rest of his army was broken up into detachments, including Bandera's troop. They were stationed with rare military skill. It was said that they could be concentrated and moved en masse within thirty-six hours. All told, the force in the province could not amount to more than 3,500 men. It was reported that Bandera had been reduced to the ranks by Gomez for issuing a distasteful proclamation to the negroes. Like a true soldier, he accepted the situation and won anew the rank of brigadier-general within a very few months.

Last of all, the Province of Santiago was canvassed. Here Calixto Garcia has been conducting operations for a long time, and he is now in complete control with headquarters at Bayamo. The only cities held by the Spaniards are Holguin, Manzanillo, and Santiago de Cuba. Garcia has a fair supply of provisions. It was the only province that escaped unscathed from Weyler's order. The Cubans control the provincial government and collect the taxes. Hundreds of Spanish prisoners are said to be employed in the mountains raising cattle and cultivating provisions for Garcia's army. The Spanish general, Pando, had been pounding away at Garcia along the Canto River for more than six months, but had finally given up the job, and was said to be in command in Cienfuegos. Garcia has a force of 7,500 men, well equipped and fairly supplied with ammunition. He has several pieces of artillery which were used with good effect in the siege of Las Tunas. The city was taken by assault and its fortifications destroyed.

From this it will be seen that Gomez is in perfect communication with every detachment of the Cuban army, and that its entire strength on the island is about 15,000 men. This is a far greater number than Gomez had when Maceo headed the magnificent march to the west.

Such was a part of the information gleaned from my Cuban visitor. It was late in the afternoon when the delegate of the junta left my room. He slipped out quietly and made his exit from the hotel by an outlet in the rear. That night I met him on the street. He was greatly agitated, and asked what had become of the printed proclamation of Gomez.

"Did you not take it away with you?" I inquired.

"Never, never," was the reply. "Is it not in your pocket?"

"No," was the answer. "It must have been left upon the table. Wait one moment and I will go and see."

Back to the hotel I went. There was a score of papers upon the table, but the proclamation was not among them. When I returned and made this report the Cuban blanched with fear. "It has been stolen by the attendant of your room," said he, "and I am lost."

"Possibly," I replied, "the Senator took it." I made inquiries of the Senator, who looked over the papers in his pocket and found it. When it was returned to its owner the latter gave a great sigh of relief. Before sundown of the succeeding day it was in the hands of General Betancourt.

HEROISM OF THE INSURGENTS.

There is a disposition to regard Gomez and his associates as little better than bandits, guerrillas, and bushwhackers, but the fact is that the Cuban patriots have never been reduced to such dire distress as were the American patriots at Valley Forge. With ample supplies of provisions, clothing, artillery, ammunition, and equipments. Gomez was confident of his ability to drive the Spaniards from the island. His men are well seasoned and amenable to discipline, and have never declined a battle with Spanish troops on equal terms.

Garcia has practically held the Province of Santiago for two years and defeated every attempt of the enemy to dislodge him. His troops are now perched upon the mountains near the city of Santiago, awaiting the opportunity for a final swoop. The Spanish army cooped within that city is as sure to be captured as was Cornwallis at Yorktown. The American fleet at Santiago will cinch the situation as perfectly as did the fleet of the Count de Grasse in the Chesapeake. Gomez has held nearly half of the province of Puerto Principe ever since Maceo's great march to the west. Weyler found it impossible to expel him and returned to Havana in disgust. Fabius himself never handled his army more adroitly in the days of Hannibal. The Cuban Government maintained itself in its mountain capital despite all efforts to disperse it.

The Continental Congress fled from Philadelphia to Annapolis in the days of the Revolution, but the Cuban Government maintains itself where it was first established. It is organized on a constitutional basis, and its legislative and executive decrees are

in a line with all republican precedents. Its President, Bartolomé
Massó, is undoubtedly already in communication with our Government. Gomez derives his authority as general the same as
Nelson A. Miles gets his authority here and is fully as amenable to
the law. In no case has the military authority ever refused to
bow to the will of the civil government. Obedience to the law is
as strongly ingrained in the Cuban army as in the American
Army. Its losses have been terrific, but the patriotic fire burns
as brightly as ever in the hearts of those who survive.

If we judge of the future by the past, there is no question of
the ability and willingness of the patriots to materially aid our
forces in their campaign of liberation. They are strengthened in
this desire by the official assurance of the President and of Congress that it is a campaign of liberation, and not one of annexation, as the Spaniards assert. The history of the war in Cuba has
never been written. The American people know as little about it
as they knew of the wholesale starvation of the reconcentrados
four months ago. It exists in fragments and fag-ends, to be
gathered by some future foreign historian, as Botta gathered the
historical débris of the American Revolution.

The revolution began on February 24, 1895. The first object of
Martinez Campos was to isolate it to the province of Santiago.
On May 1 Gomez had 600 soldiers, mostly cavalry. They were
stationed at Mejorana, about 25 miles from the city of Santiago.
With 200 of these soldiers, accompanied by José Marti, he started
for Puerto Principe to spread the insurrection. Maceo was left
behind with 400 mounted troops. He broke for Holguin, one of
the principal cities of Santiago, 20 miles from the northern coast.
The Spaniards there were thrown into a panic. They brought to
their aid the garrison of Las Tunas, 40 miles to the west. This
was what Maceo wanted. It left the way open to Gomez and his
troopers. Marti was killed in a little fight at Dos Rios and Gomez
passed safely into Puerto Principe.

Maceo promptly withdrew from Holguin and marched back to
Cauto Abajo, about 15 miles northwest of Mejorana. About this
time Martinez Campos arrived at Manzanillo, 30 miles southwest of
Bayamo. On July 12 he began his famous march to Bayamo.
Maceo on July 5 had heard that Campos was expected. Bayamo
is at least 70 miles west of Cauto Abajo. With Goulet, Masso,
Rabi, and Guerra, Maceo advanced toward Bayamo. He had
about 1,200 men, the cavalry being armed with machetes and the
infantry with everything that could be found in the shape of a
shooting iron. With these men Maceo waylaid Campos at Peralejo. The Spanish General Santocildes was killed and Campos
escaped to Bayamo without even an escort, the Spanish force
being utterly routed. Campos concentrated his forces, returned
to Manzanillo, and went back to Havana.

Meantime Gomez set Camaguey aflame with insurrection. A
constituent assembly was called, representing every province, and
a civil government established. Gomez was made commander in
chief and Maceo lieutenant-general. The mulatto general had
gone back to Banabacoa, 15 miles southeast of Cauto Abajo.
While here he received orders from Gomez to organize a column
for the invasion of the western part of the island. Havana was
nearly 500 miles away. On receiving these orders, Maceo marched
to Baragua, 10 miles north of Cauto Abajo. There he was joined
by Quintin Bandera and Luis Feria, increasing his army to 1,200
men, of which 700 were cavalry. General Gomez arrived at Ba-

ragua on October 11. On October 22 the invading column began
its march, under the direct command of Maceo. On November 1
it was joined by 500 cavalry under Generals Miro and Santana.

All this time Campos was making preparations anew to squelch
the insurrection. The Spanish official figures credit him with
172,295 men. Add to these 50,000 Spanish volunteers recruited in
Cuba and 16,000 regulars newly arrived, and his total force, allowing for losses, was not below 200,000. Campos made the mistake of underestimating the strength of the patriots. He looked
upon them as a lot of bushwhackers and was entirely unaware of
their plans. The intention was to break into Puerto Principe,
south of Las Tunas. On November 5 scouts reported 3,000 Spaniards awaiting the advancing column, 12 miles southeast of Las
Tunas.

Maceo sent General Capote, with 300 men, to make a feint on
that city. It was masterful strategy. The Spanish column tore
back to the city to defend it, and Maceo's troops rushed through
the gap. On November 7 Maceo entered Puerto Principe. Gomez
left the column with a small escort, promising to rejoin it with
reenforcements within a month. The insurrection was spreading,
and the Spanish troops, who had been flanked at Las Tunas, were
on Maceo's trail. General Echague, who commanded the pur-
suers, followed Maceo's column over a hundred miles, but finally
gave it up after numerous skirmishes and went down to the Caribbean coast, to Santa Cruz del Sur.

Maceo's forces grew in numbers as he advanced into the more
thickly populated country. By the end of November he had left
the city of Puerto Principe on his right. The eastern trocha was
only 60 miles away. This had been constructed in the ten-years
war and had been strengthened by Campos. The ditch ran from
Moron, on the northern coast, to Jucaro, on the Caribbean shore.
By this time Campos was fully awake. He had 16,000 troops along
this trocha, with a chain of blockhouses, a railroad, a telegraph
line, and ironclad cars. Echague and his troops had been brought
from Santa Cruz del Sur by steamer, and were among the 16,000
now confronting the wily mulatto. At 6 o'clock on the morning
of November 29 Maceo broke from the woods at Ciego d'Avila, 12
miles north of Jucaro, swerved to the right, and crossed the trocha
between two small forts. Before the Ciego garrison was awake
he had pried up the rails, cut the wires, and was sweeping westward like a prairie fire.

Thus the second plan of Campos to head off the insurrection
failed. The march had been through a land of forests and fields,
and the roads were little better than mountain paths. On the day
that Maceo passed the trocha Gomez joined him with General
Sanchez and General Roloff. For two days the troops remained
in camp. It was the first rest they had taken since the start.
Havana was still nearly 300 miles away. Terrible work was before them. They were about to enter a province gridironed with
railways and defended by 80,000 Spanish troops. The column had
increased until it numbered 5,000 men.

On December 2 they broke camp at dawn. Before 8 o'clock the
road was disputed. Two squadrons of cavalry swept upon the
Spanish army under Suarez Valdez, while Maceo passed his flank
and made for the boundary line between Puerto Principe and
Santa Clara. After this fight the infantry and cavalry under
Maceo separated. Quintin Bandera, with 1,000 infantry, was sent
into the valley of the Trinidad for recruits. He knew the country

thoroughly. Within ten weeks he rejoined Maceo's column near Havana with 4,000 well drilled and fairly armed patriots.

On December 3 Maceo's column crossed the Jatibonico and entered Santa Clara. Gomez led the advance. He was ambushed by a Spanish column of 800 men, under Colonel Segura. Maceo, hearing the firing, charged the Spaniards in the rear, fighting hand to hand over brush and fallen logs. Segura was routed, and the Cubans captured many arms and much ammunition.

By this time Havana began to exhibit some anxiety. Campos reassured its citizens by saying that he had planted a rat trap for Maceo. He wanted the Cuban column to enter a triangle marked by the cities of Sagua, Colon, and Cienfuegos, when he would surely annihilate it. These cities were crowded with troops and the intervening country cobwebbed with railroads. Maceo and Gomez dashed into the rat trap with their usual fury, swerving north and south, and making mysterious curves and zigzags. At Mal Tiempo on December 15 the 4,000 Cubans struck a large body of Spaniards in an immense guava plantation.

The Spaniards were commanded by Colonel Molina, now military governor of Matanzas. Maceo and Gomez promptly charged them, swinging down into a railroad cut and hacking down a wire fence. Molina three times formed a hollow square, but each time the square was broken by the Cuban cavalry, and the Spaniards finally scattered among the guava bushes and sugar cane, losing their regimental colors, 140 rifles, and 10,000 cartridges. Two hours later Maceo charged a strong Spanish column coming to the relief of Molina. This was promptly smashed, and had no sooner gone to pieces than a third column was encountered. This was dispersed with ease, the Spaniards flying in all directions. Over 8,000 Spanish troops were in these three columns.

Havana was only 130 miles away, but between it and the Cubans were 80,000 Spaniards under command of Campos. The most of these were infantry. The Spanish cavalry was worthless, and Campos had more field artillery than he could use. The Cuban general, Lacret, made a dash into the heart of Matanzas, cutting railways and burning stations. Gomez and Maceo moved into the sugar plantations and crossed the River Anabana into Matanzas. On December 21 they came upon Suarez Valdez like a thunderclap. He fled precipitately. At midnight Maceo camped at Santa Elena. In the gray of the morn he discovered a Spanish column in a grove of palms near by and quickly routed it.

Then came the most brilliant days in the history of Cuba. Gomez and Maceo were well within the triangle. Campos tried to spring his rat trap. He had gathered his troops at Colon to strike a decisive blow, but Maceo moved like a meteor. At midnight of December 22 Maceo camped within 2 miles of Colon, and Campos was sure of trapping him in the morning, but the Cuban column faded with the stars. Campos was fooled as Washington fooled Cornwallis at Trenton. Zigzag strategy was again brought into play. Carefully and stealthily Maceo threaded his way through the sugar fields in the dusk of the morn until the main road was reached, when the column once more spurred to the west. Campos was dumfounded, but acted with surprising energy. The rat trap was still open.

Telegrams to Havana and Matanzas set his whole army in motion by rail. His 7,000 troops at Colon were sent to Coliseo on the trains, where he again lay en perdu, awaiting Cuba's matchless chieftain. Then a new and portentious feature of the war sent a cold chill through his spinal marrow. A pillar of smoke arose in the south, and then another in the east, and a third in the west, and a fourth in the north, until the sun was blotted from the heavens. The sugar plantations were aflame. Meantime Gomez swept down upon Roque, while Maceo dashed for Coliseo. At Roque Gomez tapped the telegraph, which disclosed the concentration of the Spanish troops and laid bare the plans of Campos. The wires were cut and the rails were displaced, and the concentration of 40,000 troops was paralyzed. The trap remained unsprung.

Campos sweated with agony, but still retained his presence of mind. Maceo was advancing in five parallel columns. The middle column was ambuscaded by Campos in a sugar plantation. The generals were not 300 feet apart. The mulatto patriot deployed to the right and left and answered the Spanish fire. Two great wings of 4,000 men were enveloping him. His matchless genius arose to the situation. He dispatched aids to his flanking columns with orders that spoke for themselves. Within twenty-five minutes the city of Coliseo was in flames and the village of Sumidero was ablaze. One was to the east and the other to the west of Campos.

Meantime Maceo himself set the cane on fire in the immediate front of the Captain-General. Campos became hopelessly involved between three lines of flames. He sounded a retreat and put for Matanzas, fancying that it was Maceo's intention to capture that city. The victorious Cubans swept westward like avenging spirits, while clouds of smoke arising from a hundred burning plantations bewildered the Spaniards and left Campos himself dazed and apparently unconscious of what had struck him.

Then Maceo appeared at the gates of Havana. It was Christmas week. He had been nine weeks in the saddle. He maintained his position in front of Havana four months, while the whole western end of the island was wrapped in a pall of smoke, and $60,000,000 in property went to ashes. Campos never recovered his footing and was recalled to Spain. And this is only one chapter, but a glorious chapter, in the history of the efforts of the patriots to give the blessings of freedom to Cuba.

OUR LAST SUNDAY IN CUBA.

It was March 13, our last Sunday in Cuba. The day was spent in Matanzas, a city of 48,000 inhabitants. There was not a fleck in the sky. A cool breeze swept over the bay, tempering the heat of the sun. A blue haze veiled the distant mountains and brought vividly to mind the Blue Ridge of Virginia. Standing near a Spanish blockhouse on a height above the city, the lovely valley of the Yumuri lay below us on the left of the ridge, dotted with palms, seamed with silvery streams, and carpeted with the richest vegetation of the island. On the left extended the San Juan Valley, not so picturesque, but equally as fertile, stretching to the west until lost in tropical thickets, lurking places of Cuban patriots.

No forests were to be seen. The mountains are covered with scrub, so thick that it can be penetrated only by the use of a machete. It was a perfect spring day—like a day in June in New England. But the air was not filled with melody, and there were few signs of insect life. The mellow note of the robin was not heard, nor the cry of the catbird. Even the mocking bird and the blackbird were missing, and there were no shrill screechings from paroquets. No quail, no finches, no woodpeckers, no cardinals, no orioles, not even a ground chippy. The only birds to be seen were lazy buzzards and little doves not larger than wrens. The Spanish soldiers were trapping the doves and potting their tiny bodies in stews, seasoned with garlic and sweet peppers.

Near by stood a stone church, surrounded by a low wall of masonry. It was surmounted by a gilt cross and was known as the Church of the Black Virgin. The doors stood wide open, but there were no services and no rectory nor outbuildings. The altar was covered with seashells, and an image of the Black Virgin appeared above it in an artificial grotto, crucifix in hand. The church was built in the last century by a Spanish grandee to commemorate some momentous event in the history of his family. The bell in the belfry was cast over two hundred years ago. Services were held only twice a year. The yard was shaded by a row of Spanish oaks, natives of the Balearic Islands. Catalan troops were quartered in the yard and evidently intended to cut away the oaks, make embrasures in the walls, and use the place as a redoubt in case of an assault on the city. It completely commanded both town and harbor.

Standing on the wall and gazing to the southeast, a railroad train pulling out for Santa Clara, Sagua la Grande, and Cienfuegos was in full view. A trail of steam marked its windings among the blockhouses until lost to sight in the abandoned plantations on the other side of the harbor. The train was hardly out of sight before two companies of Spanish troopers entered the city not far from the railroad station. They came from the direction of Guanabana and left a cloud of dust behind them. It was afterwards ascertained that they had had a little brush with Betancourt's men near La Vieja, 5 miles southwest of Guanabana. Viewed from the Church of the Black Virgin they looked like a detachment from the bodyguard of the Queen of Liliput. They rode over the stone bridge crossing the San Juan, and disappeared in the narrow streets of the city.

Below the church on the right of the road an exquisite residence attracted attention. Its white walls gleamed in the sunlight from an embowerment of orange trees and sapodillas. Palms and oleanders shaded the inner court, and its front was aflame with the royal purple of the hibiscus. The guardia civil in our entourage, finding that one of the party spoke Spanish, became extremely talkative. The mansion, be said, was owned by a sugar planter, now in Europe. It was one of the finest residences in the province. Certainly no more sightly and healthy spot could be found. It overlooked the bay and the city, and it was fanned by cool sea breezes.

The rarest tropical fruits were propagated on its grounds, and it contained the richest furniture and an art gallery valued at a high figure. Its owner had abandoned the island in disgust. His sugar plantations had been destroyed and an income among the hundreds of thousands sent skyward in smoke and flame. Hastily gathering what was left, and thankful for the safety of his family, he had sought a peaceful retreat across the water, leaving all he possessed in Cuba to be sold. Some of his plantations had brought only $6 an acre. Three thousand acres of the finest soil for tobacco had brought only $11,000. The Matanzas mansion was absolutely valueless. He could not get even an offer for it. In the opinion of the guardia civil, an offer of $4,500 would be eagerly accepted.

A moment afterwards he was relating a queer story, which he

said was rife among the Spanish residents of Matanzas. They believed that Henry M. Flagler, of New York, had been visiting the city incognito, and had secured options on many valuable pieces of property therein, with a view to making it a great winter resort for Americans. Matanzas was nearer to the terminus of his railroad in Florida than Havana, certainly not more than fifteen hours' sail. Its beauty, salubrity, pure water, fruits, and railroad connections would make it far more desirable than Nassau, and the expenditure of two or three millions of dollars in improvements would eventually put it on a par with Nice and Riviera and make it a central winter watering place for the world.

This story passed current in Matanzas. The Spaniards regarded it as proof positive that the United States intended to annex Cuba, and used it as a lever to force those with patriotic leanings into the support of the new autonomic government. Meantime, Flagler himself was at St. Augustine, apprehensive lest a declaration of war should send a Spanish fleet to ravish the coast of Florida, and the Ponciana, Palm Beach, and Royal Palm marvels be leveled to the ground. Within two weeks afterwards the Secretary of War was strengthening the defenses of St. Augustine and sending additional companies of artillery to man the new guns.

The return to town was made after a final view of the famed Valley of the Yumuri. Near the gorge where the stream breaks from the valley into Matanzas Bay there were signs of cultivation. Two men were hoeing near the river bank. A field glass disclosed their color, but failed to record the crop they were cultivating. No one was allowed to till any ground outside the city except by order from General Molina, and these were the only men handling a hoe that had been seen since our entry into Cuba. The reconcentrados use their skeleton fingers and sticks in planting tomato vines between their squalid huts, and thank God that they are allowed even this poor privilege.

FÊTE DAY IN MATANZAS.

Down the heights rolled the volante over a winding road, the sun growing hotter every minute. We stopped to inspect a small camp of reconcentrados. The palm-leaf huts were black with age and covered with dust. They were built in the shape of an inverted V, without doors, and open front and rear. It was a camp of starving children, half naked, and squalid beyond belief. Some were mere skeletons; others were swollen in the body and limbs, dropsical affections, caused by want of proper food. On entering the camp the palms rustled as scores of chameleons darted up the huts, and a hundred of the child sufferers gathered around the visitors, surveying them mournfully and extending their tiny hands. Only the most active were among the group, each hut containing some who were unable to arise, and who lay upon the ground, open-eyed, awaiting their fate in patient resignation.

The mothers were either at the hospitals or ranging the streets of the city seeking sustenance. The heat of the sun was intense. Not a breath of air was stirring. The hot air arose from the hot road and fairly quivered in the hot sky. At the heels of the strangers were the children, heading them off at every turn, and pleading for alms. Among them was a little blonde, neatly dressed, and apparently in perfect health. She wore a gold chain around her neck, and was as pretty as an ideal picture, but was as persistent in her cries for help as those on the last verge of starvation. Before the phenomenon could be explained, a visitor threw two dozen coppers into the group. They disappeared like corn thrown among famished chickens. In an instant the rash philanthropist was surrounded and fairly mobbed. He literally had to fight his way to his volante, and the party continued its journey down the hill.

In the outskirts of the city, while passing a beautiful residence of Moorish architecture, there was a far more attractive development. From the inner court trooped four ladies in Spanish attire, wearing black silk masks. They ranged themselves upon the walk and coquettishly threw kisses at the strangers. To say that the party was astonished does not cover the situation; they were astounded. In an instant, however, one of them politely removed his hat, and the others followed suit. The ladies shouted in silvery tones, "Buenas Americanos." The carriage rolled on, and in front of a rich mansion on the opposite side of the street there was a similar performance.

Within ten minutes the streets were filled with ladies en masque. All wore the masks so familiar on harlequins in pantomimes. It was about 5 o'clock in the afternoon. As the party approached the hotel barbaric music was heard. It had a weird sound—something like the drumming of Sioux Indians before roasting a captive. On alighting at the hotel the unearthly music redoubled in volume and a motley procession turned the corner. All the saloons were open and around the tables sat Spanish officers and civilians drinking light wines and smoking cigarettes. The streets were filled with barking dogs and shouting children carrying wooden rattles. At the head of the procession marched a group of gigantic negroes, bearing aloft images, among which was a representation of the Black Virgin.

The music was monotonous and horribly discordant, but it had a barbaric rhythm, and to this rhythm the negroes kept step. They beat the ground with their heels and acted like Buffalo Bill's Indians in a ghost dance. Some were scantily arrayed, and their actions savored more of the voodoo than any other ceremony. Following this advance guard were a hundred or more men and women arrayed in variegated costumes, all wearing black silk masks. All were shouting and singing and some dancing a la Egyptienne. It was a heterogeneous crowd with no regard for order and regardless of comment. A few overenthused would leave the procession and dance around and embrace spectators on the street.

The reconcentrados shrank into the doorways and side streets as the noisy column swept past them. For once their plaintive cries were stilled, and they furtively watched the surging mob. There were horns in the crowd and all sorts of strange noises. As the day died out in the gleam of the electric lights the tumult increased. By midnight there was a regular saturnalia. Everybody was riotously merry. The procession kept in motion, and the music became so barbaric that even the dogs howled in protest. The parks and plazas were alive with frivolity. Everybody seemed to be having a great time. The masqueraders were sportive and accosted each other in terms more affectionate than polished. At times they whirled in waltzes under the palms and anon joined hands and sang loudly under the electric lights.

Whenever the procession reappeared all greeted it with loud cheers and joined in the singing. The gigantic negroes stuck to their work manfully, and the dogs moaned with agony as the music increased in power. The saloons were filled to overflowing and the consumption of light wines was enormous. With all the delirium and paroxysms there was no intoxication. Even after midnight a steady stream of carriages poured along the streets filled with masked ladies and girls, hilarious and joyful, who exchanged short comments with pedestrians and at times sent kisses right and left from the tips of their fingers. Not until near daylight did the noisy scenes subside. The American visitors sought their beds amid the turbulence, and went to sleep undisturbed by either the tooting of horns or the tintinnabulation of bells. It had been fête day in Matanzas. Its citizens had been honoring the natal day of their patron saint. Whether the Black Virgin was the patron saint or not, it was evident that she was so regarded by the negroes.

A DAY ON THE TRAIN.

On Monday. March 14, I traveled from Matanzas to Sagua la Grande. In the first-class car there were half a dozen Spanish officers, the mayor of Santa Clara, a friar, and two of Clara Barton's relief expedition on their way to Sagua la Grande and Cienfuegos. The palace car had cane seats, an unswept floor, and windows washed only in the rainy season. There was no drinking water, there were no racks, and no other conveniences. Everybody smoked, although ladies occupied seats in the car.

The Americans alone carried grips, and the Spanish officers filled the vacant seats with swords tied in buckskin bags, canes, luggage rolled in red blankets well strapped, and lunch baskets. They chatted like magpies, but lacked politeness; for when ladies entered the car at way stations they were left to shift for themselves in a search for seats, no one offering to remove the luggage, swords, and baskets of the officers. The day was hot, the sun scorching, and the interior of the car suffocating. All the windows were open, and the passengers were showered with cinders.

My colleague on the journey wore a silk hat and a four-in-hand tie, and carried a silk umbrella. The hat attracted more attention than the Representative himself, and everybody regarded the umbrella with astonishment, as no rain had fallen since October.

Wherever my colleague went he created a sensation. If he alighted at a way station, the reconcentrados stopped their plaintive pleadings as he approached and gazed at the tile as though overcome with awe. Even the friar in the car, who wore a hat that looked as though it might have been made in the days of Gil Blas, never took his eyes from the Congressman's hat. It had a fascination for him that seemed overwhelming.

The American statesman, however, seemed to be absolutely unaware of the stir created by the hat. At times he smoothed the fur with a white silk handkerchief, while the little negro porters regarded him in open-mouthed wonderment and a corporal's guard of Castilian infantry ran out of their ironclad car to view the unwonted sight. Nor did his umbrella remain inconspicuous. It got mixed up with the sabers of the Spanish officials, dropped to the floor every half hour, and finally tripped the Congressman himself, nearly throwing him from the train. The monk evidently considered it a fit traveling companion for the hat.

He fanned himself for an hour or more and dropped asleep. He awoke as the train stopped at Limonar. Here a gigantic negro, half naked, entered the car and began to sell tickets in the Havana lottery. The alcalde of Santa Clara was his first customer, and the military men were eager purchasers. Last of all came the padre.

He selected his ticket with much care, paid for it in paper money, something like the old American postal currency, drew out a book of prayers in Latin, whispered languidly over it for five minutes, and again fell asleep.

At Jovellanos the Spanish guard on the platform of the depot came to an order arms as the passengers descended from the train. The Americans fancied that an arrest was about to be made, but the guard remained as motionless as statues, while the corporal in command whirled himself among the crowd and finally delivered a telegram to an officer, who did not trouble himself to return his salute. Jovellanos was a lively place, and the hackmen were as noisy and demonstrative as those in a New England town. Against the side of the depot, fronting the platform, there was a bar 20 feet long. It was quickly besieged, and the demand for lemonade, limewater, and light wines was immense.

The tumblers used in concocting lemonade would shame a weiss-beer glass. They held nearly a quart, but it was circus lemonade, circumscribed as to ice. Behind the bar there was a formidable array of bottles on a dozen shelves that would tempt the appetite of a connoisseur in wines. There was Chateau Yquem of various ages, Chateau Margaux, Perez sherry, old port, and Madeira—almost everything, in fact, outside of blue seal royal Johannesburger; but the gem of the collection was old Otard brandy, purporting to have been made in 1800, and retailed at $1 a bottle in silver. When the train from Cardenas arrived and was joined by one from Guines, on the Pinar del Rio road, the crush on the platform was terrific.

The reconcentrados shrank from the crowd, fearing an application of the canes of the Spanish officers. Aside from this, the alcalde of the city was present, wielding a gold-tipped baton of ebony, his insignia of office, and directing the guardia civile to keep the starving women and children at a distance. He was an appointee of the new autonomist cabinet, and he greeted the mayor of Santa Clara with true official courtesy. They drank together with much unction, and finally each paid for his own drink.

As the train moved out the famished Cubans lined the track beyond the station, pleading mutely but pitifully for food. Not long afterwards a ruined sugar plantation was passed. The blackened chimneys stood near the track, surrounded by a fence of driven piles, fashioned from royal palms. Under the action of the sun the piles had become as white as snow. They looked as though they had had a coat of whitewash. The whole country was a desolate waste, barring a wild, tropical outgrowth. There were hedges of Spanish bayonets and roadways shaded for miles by lofty palms, but no signs of cultivation.

Neither hut nor hacienda was to be seen, and no living animal. Even the birds had left the country, and where the soil was not blackened by fire it was flecked by the moving shadows of buzzards on the wing. The only evidences of occupation were the Spanish blockhouses that appeared on nearly every elevation. To the south arose the blue range of the Quimbambas, patched with light-gray chaparral, at the foot of which the daring Maceo turned the flank of Martinez Campos less than three years ago. The country was rolling and seamed with small streams of running water.

As the train approached the town of Cervantes the padre aroused himself from his lethargy, closed his Latin prayer book, and lighted a cigarette. Later on he opened a lunch basket and filled the car with the flavor of cold boiled ham. He had bought sapadilloes, pomegranates, and pawpaws at Jovellanos, and he regaled himself thoroughly by drinking a pint of claret snugly ensconced among the goodies in the basket. While at Cervantes a boy came up to the car, offering for sale a string of tiny fluttering birds. Their legs were tied and they were no larger than wrens.

I leaned out of the window and bought the string for a peseta. The birds resembled the mourning doves so common in Florida, although they were much smaller. They struggled for freedom as they lay in my lap and savagely pecked at my fingers. There were at least a dozen of them. I drew out my pocketknife and tried to liberate them, but their legs and feet were so closely interwoven that the knife was useless. Thereupon I summoned all my patience and deliberately began to untie the twine. The Spanish officers watched my movements with evident interest.

Within twenty minutes one of the tiny captives was free. As he darted over the priest's hat and out of the door, I shouted, "Go to Gomez." The officers looked glum. They evidently understood the words and were in no laughable mood. Each bird was tied separately and all were knotted together with the same cord. Five minutes elapsed before the second victim was released. "Go to Garcia!" I shouted, and it shot out of an open window before the faces of the officials of the Queen Regent. One young lieutenant in a rich uniform smiled, and the mayor of Santa Clara laughed outright, but the older officers moved uneasily in their seats and looked very grave. A third bird was released, with instructions to "Go to Bermudez." No one smiled.

I had unconsciously touched an exceedingly sensitive military nerve, and a "carraho," vengefully uttered, indicated that I was treading on dangerous ground.

It was a warning heeded by the interpreter, who was seated at my side. In a low tone he said that Bermudez was raiding Santa Clara, and that he had recently executed a Spanish colonel who had tried to seduce him from his allegiance to the Cuban Republic. Indignation blazed from the eyes of the officers, who awaited the flight of the fourth captive. It was freed in silence, and remained in the car some time before it found its way to the outer world. The Spaniards were still in an ill mood, and furtively watched every movement. As the bonds of the last bird were loosed and it wafted itself into the sunshine the train entered Colon. Most of the officers were at their journey's end, but the war cloud was not dispelled. Enough remained to chill the atmosphere of good-fellowship.

The friar resumed his Latin breviary, and the new military passengers were quickly informed of what had happened. I lighted a cigar and listened to the interpreter's reminiscences of the ten years' war until the boundary line was crossed and the train stopped at Mordazo. It was a small town, but death was in the air. The reconcentrados were absolutely without food or shelter and were dying like sheep in a rinderpest. A few lay in the hot sun, starving and naked, awaiting the end in utter despair.

At 3 o'clock Santo Domingo was reached. It was a little place of 800 inhabitants, where 2,700 victims of Weyler's brutality had died within three months. Here the destination of the party was changed.

A dispatch from Sagua was received announcing the sudden

death of the wife of Senator THURSTON. Her death took us to
Sagua la Grande instead of Santa Clara. There were three trains
at the station—one bound for Cienfuegos, a second for Santa
Clara, and a third for Sagua. Misled in the confusion, I boarded
the wrong train. It was moving out of the station when I discovered my mistake. I sprang from the platform, satchel in
hand, and made a break for the Sagua train. Too late—it was
disappearing around a curve, leaving a trail of black smoke behind it. In an instant I realized the utter loneliness of my situation. Here I was in the interior of Cuba, in a small country
town, unable to make myself understood and unable to understand others. I felt like a man dumped on the Sahara Desert
miles from any oasis. Not a railroad employee understood a word
of English. All I could say was "Sagua." "Sagua?" repeated
the ticket agent, and shook his head. All the trains had gone,
and there were none to follow them until the succeeding day.
There was no railroad service at night because of the activity of
the insurgents.

While standing absorbed in a quandary, a reconcentrado appeared before me. He was gaunt and thin, but his ragged rai-
ment was clean. He divined the situation like a flash. Pointing
to the northeast, he imitated the puffing of a locomotive and
placed the fingers of his right hand in the palm of his left. I
took the hint. The train had stopped around the curve, and the
reconcentrado began to run up the track in the hot sunlight. I
followed him at a dead jump. The rear of the train was quickly
in sight. It had stopped at a grade crossing a quarter of a mile
away. Before I could reach it it was off again. I waved my
hat, but there was no response.

There was a wine shop filled with Spanish soldiers at the grade
crossing. They regarded me with much curiosity as I entered the
shop. Waving my hand toward them, I shouted "Vinos!" and
silently invited them to drink. They eagerly accepted the invitation, and half a dozen bottles of light wine were placed on the
tables. The soldiers were Gallegos. They sympathized with me,
but were utterly unable to give me any information. Meantime
my interpreter appeared. Missing me, he had sprung from the
train, and had come back to spend the night with me. He reported
that the conductor was about to hold the train when he saw me
running toward it, but the Spanish officers interfered. They
had not forgotten the liberation of the birds. "Let him go to
Gomez!" and "Let him go to Bermudez!" they cried. They
alluded to me as an "American pig," and said that the walking
to Sagua la Grande was good. The interpreter warned the conductor that he would have to return when the train reached
Sagua, as the belated passenger was a Federal deputy, and the
Span sh officers roared with laughter. The conductor refused to
stop, and the train sped on.

After a parting glass with the Gallegos, the interpreter and myself held a council of war. A dispatch was sent to Consul Barker
at Sagua la Grande, informing him that I had missed the train
and would come up to Sagua on the following day. Then the
mayor was sought. He kept the only drug store in the town, and
received his visitors rather coldly. We left him and entered a
little restaurant on the corner. It was reeking with garlic and
the fare was limited, but the proprietor was urbane and attentive
and the wine excellent.

After dinner we sought the priest in a search for lodging. As

3543—4

we were crossing the plaza toward the cathedral, the mayor appeared with his baton of office and urged us not to go near the priest. He said that the padre was a bitter Spaniard and that we would be driven from his door with contempt. I. however, persisted, and was received with the most cordial hospitality. While conversing with the priest the station agent arrived with a dispatch announcing that a special train had left Sagua in search of the lost Federal deputy. At the same moment the wh'stle of the locomotive was heard. The priest parted with his visitors apparently with sincere regret. We boarded the train, saluted the chagrined conductor, and arrived at Sagua at dark. There Consul Barker warmly greeted us and conducted us to the hotel, amid hundreds of starving reconcentrados Two days afterwards we received a health certificate from the health officer at Havana, departe 1 on a New Orleans steamer. and landed at Key West the next morning, thanking God that we were once again under the Stars and Stripes.

These, Mr. Chairman, are a few of the experiences of the Congressional delegation that visited Cuba in March. I have not dwelt upon the number of reconcentrados who were starved to death, because these were fully detailed in the statements of the visiting Senators, and I fully agree with them. At the least, over 200,000 persons had died of starvation under the Weyler or ier when we left Cuba. This order was rescinded by General Blanco a week before the declaration of war. Since then the sufferers must have been nearly exterminated. Whatever food was left by Miss Clara Barton for their support was seized by the Span.ards, and death has undoubtedly performed its work unchallenged.

3513

O

www.ingramcontent.com/pod-product-compliance
Lightning Source LLC
Chambersburg PA
CBHW030904260626
47169CB00008B/2678